Coincidence

ALSO BY ELAINE NOONE

Jersey Squall

Coincidence

A Novel

By

ELAINE NOONE

Wintervane Publications
Manasquan, New Jersey 08736

Wintervane Publications
P.O. Box G
Manasquan, New Jersey 08736

PUBLISHER'S NOTE

This is a work of fiction. Names, characters, places, and incidents are either the product of the author's imagination or are used fictitiously. Any resemblance to actual persons, living or dead, business establishments, events, or locales is entirely coincidental.

ISBN 978-0-9828265-1-5
Library of Congress Control Number: 2021905404

Wintervane Publications
Manasquan, New Jersey 08736

To my seat mates,
And, to Sam, who told me a story

Coincidence:

1 a remarkable concurrence of events or circumstances without apparent causal connection.

2 correspondence in nature or in time of occurrence.

--The Oxford American College Dictionary
The Oxford University Press, Inc., 2002

Coincidence

Morgan Prince

~ 1 ~

Las Vegas, Nevada

It was the last day of the Consumer Electronics Show in Las Vegas. Morgan Prince took the elevator down to the lobby of the MGM Hotel. He had two appointments scheduled for the morning at the Las Vegas Convention Center.

Prince stepped off the elevator and was immediately accosted by a beautiful red-haired woman. The woman took his arm and guided him to the narrow passageway beyond the elevator. She whispered in his ear. She held Prince's arm as they walked back to the elevator bank.

Prince and the woman boarded. Prince pressed his floor.

At 8:45 a.m. that morning, the beautiful red-haired woman called down to the reception desk to report that the guest in Room 559 was in need of medical assistance.

She propped open the door to the hotel room with the USA Today newspaper that lay on the carpet in the corridor.

The beautiful red-haired woman disappeared.

~ 2 ~

Las Vegas Hospital, Las Vegas, Nevada

Morgan Prince underwent an immediate quadruple bypass procedure at Las Vegas Hospital. After almost six hours in the operating room, Prince's surgeon had closed him up. The heart monitor recorded a steady heart beat.

"Thanks, everyone." The surgeon stepped back from the operating table.

Prince's body jerked on the table.

The heart monitor began to beep erratically.

Prince went into cardiac arrest.

Pandemonium broke out in the operating room. The doctors and nurses scrambled to save him.

The surgeon reopened the incision on Prince's chest.

"We're losing him! We're losing him!" cried the surgeon. "C,mon, folks! Let's do this!"

The heart monitor flat-lined.

There was silence in the room. The surgical team stared at the monitor.

The surgeon shook his head.

"Time of death, 2:39 p.m."

Morgan Prince stared down at the group of exhausted doctors and nurses in the operating room. He squinted down at his own body lying on the table below him. Prince glanced away.

He saw the pink sky of a beautiful sunset in the distance. He followed a sandy path to a dune. The sky was a fiery red when Prince reached the top of the dune. He took a step down the dune toward the ocean.

He heard a voice calling to him.

"Daddy! Daddy, come back!"

Prince knew that voice. It belonged to Alicia, the younger of his two girls. Prince looked around for her.

"Daddy, come back. This way! Come this way!"

Prince turned in the direction of his daughter's voice. He took a step back up to the top of the dune.

Prince found himself back in the operating room. He floated back down into his body.

The heart monitor began to beep. Its screen displayed the steady rhythm of Prince's heartbeat.

Prince's surgeon stopped during his evening rounds.

"How are you feeling this evening, Mr. Prince?"

"It feels like there's a big weight on my chest," said Prince, his voice hoarse and raspy.

The doctor nodded. "That's normal. It will go away. How's your breathing?"

"It hurts some," said Prince.

The surgeon nodded.

"Your heart attack walloped your body, Mr. Prince. It will take some time for everything to get back to normal."

The surgeon checked Prince's chart. "Everything looks good," he said. He shook his head.

"You gave us quite a scare this morning," he said.

Prince squinted at the doctor.

"Did I die?"

The surgeon hesitated.

"Doctor, I heard you call my death," said Prince. "Time of death, 2:39 p.m."

The surgeon hesitated.

"The procedure was a success," said the surgeon. "We started your heart again and all your signs looked good. I closed you up," he said. "And then your heart stopped."

"I saw it," said Prince. "I heard you call my death."

The surgeon squinted at him, shaking his head.

"I saw everyone in a panic in the operating room," said Prince. "I turned away and saw the bright light of a sunset in the distance. I started walking toward it, but I heard my daughter's voice calling me back. I floated back into my body."

"Suddenly, your heart started to beat again," said the doctor, "and all your signs were normal. It was one of the damnedest things I've ever seen."

"It was one of the strangest experiences I've ever had," said Prince.

"Well, Mr. Prince, I'm very happy that you came back," said the surgeon. "Welcome back. Count yourself among the lucky."

~ 3 ~

San Diego, California

Marie Prince had her husband transferred from Las Vegas Hospital to San Diego Regional, closer to their home.

Marie sat by her husband's bedside and researched physical rehabilitation facilities for him once he was released from the hospital. She arranged for his admittance into an inpatient treatment program in San Diego.

Marie encouraged him in his recovery.

On the day of his release from rehab, Marie picked him up. She prepared a heart-healthy dinner for his homecoming. Their two girls, Gwen and Alicia, happily chattered at the dinner table.

Morgan and Marie put the girls to bed together.

They watched a movie together in the den. When the movie ended, Marie reminded Morgan of his doctor's orders to get his rest. She sent him to bed. She fell asleep on the couch in the den.

Morgan joined the girls for breakfast before they left for school. Marie sat across from him at the table, drinking a cup of coffee.

The girls chattered happily to their father.

Prince walked the girls to the bus stop after breakfast. He returned home to find Marie still sitting at the table.

"Wow, I'm winded from just that short walk to the bus stop," said Morgan. "I guess I've got a long way to go."

"You just have to work at it, Morgan," said Marie. "Faithfully." She drummed her fingers on the table.

"Marie, I'm sorry. I wish this had never happened."

"Of course you do, Morgan," scoffed Marie. "You got caught."

"No, Marie. I had a moment of insanity," said Morgan. "It's insane for me to jeopardize what I have with you and the girls. I'm sorry."

Marie frowned.

"Marie, can we get past this?" said Morgan.

"Maybe we can, in time," said Marie, shaking her head. She got up from the table and carried her coffee cup to the sink.

"Marie, I know I made a huge mistake," said Morgan. "Will you accept my apology? Won't you please give me another chance? It will never happen again. Please believe me."

"Morgan, I do believe you," said Marie. "I'm afraid it's just too late."

"Why is it too late, Marie?"

"Excuse me," said Marie.

Marie left the room and returned with a manila folder in her hand. She placed it on the table and pushed it in front of her husband.

"Morgan, since your heart attack, I've had a lot of time to think about our marriage," said Marie. "And I'm afraid that I've found our marriage lacking. I think that it's time for us to explore life apart."

Prince opened the folder. On his first full day home from rehab, Marie had served him with divorce papers.

Marie's lawyer argued successfully that Marie be awarded full custody of the girls in the divorce. Her lawyer cited Prince's health crisis, his frequent travel for work, and, at the time of the divorce, his lack of stable employment. Since his recuperation from his heart attack, Prince derived his income from freelance consulting for tech companies.

Awarded full custody of the girls, Marie took them cross-country, from California, to New York City. Morgan remained in the family home in San Diego.

The girls spent the first two summers with him at the family home. The following year, they went to camp, and that became their summer tradition.

Prince communicated via video chats with his daughters but it was hard for him to maintain relevance in his daughter's lives from such a distance. The girls were growing up. They had activities and social lives of their own.

When Marie began to date Dan, an optometrist, the girls chattered to Morgan about Dan's boat and his house in the Hamptons. When Marie and Dan married, she and the girls moved into Dan's home in Greenwich Village.

Prince's communications with his daughters became increasingly stilted and awkward. He decreased the frequency of his contact with the girls.

He let his communication lapse further.

A year passed, then another.

Over time, Prince had lost all contact with his girls.

~ 4 ~

San Diego, California

The coffeehouse on Genesee Avenue in San Diego bustled with activity as students and businesspeople streamed in and out during the morning coffee rush. Morgan Prince worked at a table near the door, his laptop open on the table in front of him.

Morgan Prince was between jobs. His employment with a mobile printer company in San Diego had ended when the firm reduced staff due to slow revenues. Prince had resumed working as an independent consultant. Freelancing paid the bills as he searched for a new full-time position.

Prince read questions from a client about a presentation he had delivered the day before.

'Are you suggesting that design is more important than quality?'

Prince typed his response.

'A certain level of quality is required to meet basic user expectations, but innovative design offers a significant opportunity to cut through the multitude of products competing for the same consumer.'

A new e-mail arrived in Prince's in-box from the talent recruiter at Audio Designs in New York City. Prince opened the e-mail. The message disappointed him.

'Our open position has been filled by another qualified candidate. We will keep your résumé on file for one year, to be considered for other relevant opportunities.'

Prince had hoped to get an employment offer from the firm. He frowned. He read the next question from his client.

A nattily dressed man wearing a charcoal gray suit with a gray and white striped tie approached Prince's table.

"Excuse me. May I sit here?" the man asked. He pointed to the empty chair at Prince's table. "I'm afraid that there are no empty tables this morning. Do you mind?"

"Not at all," said Prince. He pulled back folders to clear space on the table for the man.

"Thank you. Good morning. I'm David Bromwell."

"Good morning. I'm Morgan Prince."

Mr. Bromwell's phone buzzed.

"Good morning, Krista," Mr. Bromwell answered. "What have you got?" He listened.

"Hmm," he said, "that last candidate sounds like she might be a possibility. Why don't you set something up?" He ended the call.

"I'm sorry for the interruption," said Mr. Bromwell. "I'm hiring for a few open positions at my firm. It seems that interviewing candidates is almost a full-time job in itself."

"I'm the flip side of that coin," said Prince, nodding. "I'm searching for a position."

Mr. Bromwell glanced at Prince's open laptop. "But you appear to be working."

"I am," said Prince. "I'm an independent consultant. I'm searching for a full-time position with a technology company."

"Why is that?" asked Mr. Bromwell. "I'd think there

would be a lot of freedom in working for yourself."

"There is," said Prince, nodding, "and that's something that I like about consulting. I've been able to fall back on it when I'm between jobs, like now."

"What don't you like about it?" asked Mr. Bromwell.

"I don't enjoy the constant hustle for clients," said Prince. "Consulting doesn't offer the security of a full-time job with an employer."

"I suppose that's true," said Mr. Bromwell. "Well, how many clients do you currently have?"

"Two, at the moment," said Prince.

"You must be competent at what you do."

"I've had a lot of experience," said Prince.

"Ah," said Mr. Bromwell, nodding.

"Can I ask what line of work you're in?" Prince asked.

"I run a security outfit," said Mr. Bromwell. "My firm deploys state of the art technology to provide the highest level of protection in the industry."

"That sounds impressive," said Prince. "Security," he said. "Does that mean Brinks trucks? Banks? Jewelry stores?"

"No. Most of the firm's work is in protecting individual clients," said Mr. Bromwell.

"Oh, I see," said Prince. "Personal protection."

"Yes. Mr. Prince, perhaps it's serendipity that we met today," said Mr. Bromwell. "You're searching for a full-time position and I'm searching for a candidate to fill a position at my firm. Perhaps you should apply for my open position."

Prince smiled. "I'm afraid that I have no experience in the security field. My background is in marketing."

"The firm offers training," said Mr. Bromwell. "In the security business, events don't always unfold the way we expect. Sometimes, physical techniques are required for success."

"I see," said Prince.

"Mr. Prince, might you consider a change in career? I'd really like to fill a position."

Mr. Bromwell gave his business card to Prince.

Two italicized red letters, 'A' and 'S', were centered on a glossy black background on the front of the card. Prince turned the card over and read the contact information on the back.

"If you call the number on the back, my assistant Krista will set up an appointment for us to talk further."

"Mr. Bromwell, that's very generous of you," said Prince.

Mr. Bromwell stood up from the table.

"It was a pleasure meeting you, Mr. Prince."

"Thank you for the opportunity," said Prince. "I'm glad that you sat down at my table today."

"As am I," said Mr. Bromwell. "I'm thrilled at the coincidence of our meeting. Thank you for the conversation."

~ 5 ~
La Jolla, California

Morgan Prince sat on the balcony of his La Jolla condo on New Year's Eve. He had returned from a job with Ascenda Security in New Mexico that afternoon. Prince had no plans to celebrate the new year. He watched the moon rise in the night sky.

Prince pulled out his personal phone and scrolled through his list of contacts. He stared down at his daughter Gwen's cell phone number. It had been several years since he had dialed it. He didn't know if the number was still active.

He tapped the number.

He hit the 'Call' button.

The phone began to ring.

Prince hung up before the call was answered.

Samantha Baker

~ 1 ~
Charlotte, North Carolina

Samantha Baker met Kip Fields at a movie theater on a sweltering July day. Kip had struck up a conversation with her while the two waited to buy tickets for the afternoon show. They had laughed together over their eagerness to get out of the hot summer sun and into the cool darkness of an air-conditioned movie theater. Samantha had accepted Kip's invitation to accompany him to a nearby air-conditioned diner for dessert after the show.

Three years later, Samantha had ended the lease on her apartment in Charlotte and was moving into Kip's condo in Uptown Charlotte. She watched the sun set from the floor-to-ceiling windows of the living room before unpacking the last of her boxes.

Samantha unwrapped the orange bubble wrap around a framed photograph that had been taken by Kip's former college roommate, Bill, on a fishing trip off the Outer Banks. In the photo, Samantha leaned against Kip as the two laughed together. Kip could always make her laugh.

Samantha placed the picture over the mantle of her new home.

~ 2 ~
Las Vegas, Nevada

Samantha took the monorail from the MGM Hotel to the Flamingo and Caesars Palace Station in Las Vegas. It was Samantha's first trip to the city. She had accompanied Kip on a business trip.

Samantha had spent the day sightseeing while Kip attended his industry's annual show at the Las Vegas Convention Center. The two had arranged to meet at the Flamingo Hotel when Kip finished his work duties for the day.

Samantha found Kip waiting for her at the entrance to the garden behind the hotel. He took her arm and escorted her along the garden path. They looked for turtles from a bridge over the pond. They watched koi dart about in the water. They walked to the gazebo chapel at the end of the garden path.

A white paper carpet ran up the aisle between ten rows of empty white folding chairs. Large white bows were tied to the backs of the chairs.

Kip escorted Samantha up the aisle.

They stood in the gazebo chapel, facing the rows of empty white folding chairs.

Kip knelt down and offered her a ring.

~ 3 ~
Long Island, New York

Samantha and Kip spent the week between Christmas and New Year's in New York City, their first trip together since their engagement in Las Vegas.

The two spent their days sightseeing and their nights dining at restaurants that had been recommended to them by friends and colleagues. After dinner, they strolled arm in arm along the river. Each day, they laughed together.

Samantha and Kip had accepted an invitation to a New Year's Eve party in the Hamptons hosted by Kip's former college roommate Bill. Samantha had been reluctant to interrupt the magical time that she and Kip had enjoyed together during their week in the city but she had agreed to go after seeing Kip's eagerness to attend.

On the last night of their New York City vacation, Samantha and Kip rented a Zipcar and drove east on Long Island.

Samantha and Kip joined Bill's party guests in a champagne toast at midnight. They blew noisemakers and sang "*Auld Lang*

Syne."

The party began to break up at half past the hour.

Samantha eyed the guests as they departed at the door.

"Kip, let's go back to the city tonight," she said.

"What? We accepted Bill's invitation to stay overnight."

"Bill will understand," said Samantha. "Let's wake up in the city on our last day of vacation."

Kip shook his head. "It's a bad night to be on the roads, Sam. Anyway, I'm too drunk to drive."

"I'm not," said Samantha. "I'll drive."

"Come on, Sam. Let's just celebrate here tonight. We can go back to the city as early as you want in the morning."

The two argued.

Bill tossed Kip his coat.

"Go," he said.

Kip was asleep in the passenger seat when Samantha pulled the small Zipcar onto the westbound lanes of the Sunrise Highway.

Samantha stopped at a traffic light on the highway. She slowly accelerated when the light turned green.

The driver of a red Hummer ran his red light and broadsided the small Zipcar. The Hummer plowed the Zipcar through the intersection and slammed it into a concrete barrier on the eastbound side of the highway. The Hummer crushed the passenger side of the small vehicle before it stopped.

Samantha was thrown forward into the car's windshield. Shards of glass sliced into her head. The car's airbag pushed her back against the seat. Her head hit the head rest and bounced forward.

The Zipcar's horn sounded as Samantha slumped over the steering wheel.

~ 4 ~
Santa Barbara, California

Samantha lay in a coma in a long-term care facility in Santa Barbara, California. Five months had passed since her accident.

After spending a month in the trauma center in New York, Samantha's mother Peggy and Peggy's husband Stanley had arranged a transfer for Samantha to a facility near their home in Santa Barbara. Peggy and Stanley visited Samantha together until Stanley passed away unexpectedly two months after the transfer.

Peggy continued her daily visits to see Samantha. She sat on a vinyl chair and twisted her fingers together as she stared down at her sleeping daughter.

"Samantha, I need to say a few things. I should have said this a long time ago. I'm sorry I wasn't a better mother to you." Peggy paused.

"I apologize for making important decisions without consulting you or your sister," said Peggy. "Like selling the house after your father died. I took away your home. I'm sorry."

Peggy stared at her silent daughter.

"I just couldn't live in that house anymore without Randolph. There were just too many memories," she said, shaking her head. "And, when Josie died, it was the same thing. I couldn't live in that apartment without her. Too many damn memories."

Peggy sighed. "I'm sorry for taking away your home," she said. "Though, unfortunately, it didn't end there. I did it again when you left for college. I ended the lease on our apartment, and I moved in with Gerald," she said. "And, when you moved back home after your college graduation, I moved here, to Santa Barbara, with Stanley." Peggy frowned. "I'm sorry."

"Samantha, I'm sorry I was so careless with you," Peggy whispered.

"Good afternoon, Mrs. Larson," said Doctor Jackson. "I'd like to introduce you to a few folks. This is Ben Lewis, the administrator of our facility. Jeanne Simmons is the head of our nursing staff. John Breem is our Legal Counsel."

"What's this about?" said Peggy.

"Mrs. Larson," said Dr. Jackson, "your daughter has been in a coma for five months. Since her transfer here, we haven't observed any signs of improvement in her condition."

"But she's breathing on her own," said Peggy. "That's a good sign."

"Yes. We were surprised when your daughter started breathing on her own after we removed the ventilator," said Jackson. "However, we're not detecting normal brain activity. Your daughter appears to be in a persistent vegetative state," he said. "I'm afraid that, even if your daughter should wake from the coma, which seems unlikely, she will have significant brain damage."

Peggy inhaled sharply.

"Mrs. Larson," said the doctor, "do you wish to continue to deliver nutrients and fluids to your daughter?"

Peggy stared at the doctor. She shook her head.

"You're asking me if I want to end my daughter's life?" Peggy glared across the table.

"Mrs. Larson, we don't have to decide anything today," said Dr. Jackson.

Peggy stood from the table, shaking her head. Tears filled her eyes. She left the room.

Peggy found a rest room nearby and stood in front of the bathroom mirror, blinking back tears.

A nurse replaced Samantha's IV bag.

"Wake up, sleepyhead," the nurse whispered.

Samantha's eyes opened.

The nurse gasped. She stared down at Samantha.

"Ms. Baker, can you hear me?"

Samantha's eyes found the nurse's.

"Hi. I'm your nurse. I'm so glad you're awake."

Samantha opened her mouth to speak but no sound came out.

"Your voice hasn't been used in a while," said the nurse. "Don't worry. It will come back. Let me get the doctor."

The nurse hurried out of the room.

Peggy stepped out of the elevator onto the floor as the nurse reached the nursing station.

"Mrs. Larson!" the nurse called to her. "She's awake! Your daughter's awake! It's a miracle! Go see! I'm calling the doctor!"

Peggy entered Samantha's hospital room. She stood next to her daughter's bed. She stared down at her daughter.

Samantha's eyes were closed.

"Samantha?" Peggy whispered. "Are you awake?"

Samantha's eyes opened.

Doctor Jackson stopped by Samantha's hospital room with the results of a battery of tests he had ordered after she had awakened from the coma.

"Ms. Baker," said the doctor, "it appears that your brain function is normal," he said, staring at the report. "There is no evidence of any brain damage. It's remarkable," he said.

"Of course, you'll need physical rehab. Lying in bed for so long takes a toll on the body. But, otherwise, everything looks good. Your speech is back. Your memory is intact. You're very lucky, Ms. Baker."

"Thank you, Doctor," said Peggy. "That's good news."

"I'll check in on you again, Ms. Baker." The doctor left the room.

Samantha frowned. "He gave up on me," she said, her voice hoarse and raspy.

"What do you mean?" Peggy asked.

"I saw you in the meeting with the doctor when I was in the coma," said Samantha. "I saw you crying in the bathroom after the meeting."

"Samantha, honey," said Peggy, "I don't understand."

"I don't either," said Samantha. "But I saw a lot of things when I was in the coma. I saw you in the meeting. Was that real?"

"Yes," said Peggy. "That was real. The doctor asked if I wanted to stop your IV and feeding tubes. I was so upset." Peggy sighed. "Then I came up to visit you and the nurse told me you were awake. I was so happy."

"So, that was real," said Samantha, nodding her head. "I saw Kip standing over there next to the window and heard him calling to me, telling me to wake up," she said. "Unfortunately, that wasn't real."

"I'm sorry, Samantha," said Peggy.

"Thanks, Mom," said Samantha. She squinted, remembering. "I saw Stanley, too, when I was in the coma," she said.

"You saw Stanley?" said Peggy.

"Yes. He was wearing a yellow golf sweater. He joked that he was feeling under par."

"Stanley loved that yellow sweater," said Peggy. She paused. "Honey," she said, softly, "Stanley passed away while you were in the coma."

Samantha stared at her mother. She shook her head.

"He went peacefully in his sleep," said Peggy. "I buried him in that yellow golf sweater."

"I'm so sorry, Mom."

"Thank you, Samantha," said Peggy. "Stanley and I had a good life together. I miss him."

"So, when I saw him," said Samantha, "he was gone? Was it just a dream?"

"I don't know, honey," said Peggy.

"He apologized to me for taking you to California," said Samantha. "He told me that he loved you so much that he couldn't live without you."

"Oh, Samantha, that's a lovely thought," said Peggy.

"He gave me a message for you," said Samantha.

"Stanley gave you a message?" said Peggy.

"Yes. He said that the key to the vault is in the toe of his red slippers. Does that make any sense to you?"

"Oh, my, yes," said Peggy. "I've been searching all over for that key. In his slippers? Could it really be?"

"That's what he said."

"Well, I'll check when I go home," said Peggy. "Imagine if it's there."

"Mom, I'm sorry that Stanley's gone. I guess we're both alone now."

"We have each other," said Peggy. "And we have our memories."

Samantha squinted at Peggy.

"Too many memories," she whispered. "Too many damn memories. I heard you say that, Mom. Was that real?"

"You heard that?" said Peggy.

"Did you say that you were careless with me?" Samantha whispered.

Peggy entered Samantha's hospital room the next afternoon. She dangled a key in front of her.

"Well, Samantha, I don't understand it," said Peggy, "but it's just like you said. I found this key in Stanley's red slippers. Sure enough, it opened the vault. He also left a note."

Peggy read it aloud.

"My dear Peggy, if you're reading this, I'm sorry that I'm no longer with you. Please know that I loved you dearly. You brought such joy into my life. My only regret is that I took you away from your daughter. I loved you too much to live without you."

"So, it was real," Samantha whispered.

~ 5 ~

Santa Barbara, California

Samantha stayed with her mother in the hills of Santa Barbara after her release from the rehab facility. She drank coffee one afternoon on her mother's terrace. The screen door announced Peggy's presence.

"Good afternoon, Samantha."

"Hi, Mom. Where are you coming from?"

"A town council meeting."

"How did it go?"

"Oh, nothing was decided," said Peggy. "They're meeting again next week."

"I guess that's good," said Samantha.

"It keeps me busy," said Peggy.

A bird squawked high up in a tree.

"That reminds me," said Peggy. "I got this for you." She reached into a bag and handed a book to Samantha.

"It's a bird book," said Samantha, flipping through the colored pages that identified birds.

"You spend so much time out here that you might as well get to know the birds," said Peggy. "Stanley knew all the birds. I think that maybe you and he share that affinity."

One morning after breakfast, Samantha held up the dog-eared bird book.

"Mom, I think it's time for me to go home," she said.

"Are you sure, Samantha? It seems too soon."

"Mom, I've completed rehab," said Samantha. "The doctor says I'm healthy. I think it's time I got on with my life."

"I can come with you," said Peggy. "I can stay with you for a while."

"I think I need to do this alone, Mom. I think I'm ready."

"Are you sure?" said Peggy.

"It's time," said Samantha.

"Well, I'm going to miss having you here, Samantha," said Peggy.

"I'll miss you, too, Mom, " said Samantha. "Thanks for not giving up on me."

~ 6 ~

Charlotte, North Carolina

Samantha's hand shook as she turned the key in the lock of the Uptown Charlotte condo. She pushed the door open and stared inside before entering.

Samantha stepped inside.

She felt the quiet emptiness of the place.

She shivered.

She couldn't live there without Kip.

Samantha packed up the condo.

She moved the things that she wanted to keep into an apartment near the Coliseum.

She arranged for the delivery of Kip's personal belongings to his parents' house. She neglected to notify Kip's parents that the truck was on the way.

Jamal Williams

~ 1 ~

Freeport, New York

Seventeen-year-old Noory Turner carried a gallon of milk in one hand and a bag of groceries in the other. She climbed the steps to the landing of her mother's apartment.

Noory's pregnant belly prevented her from seeing the skateboard left out on the landing by the neighbor's children. Noory stepped onto one end of the skateboard. The opposite end flipped up, tossing Noory off balance. She fell backwards.

Noory dropped the groceries. The plastic jug of milk split as it hit the steps. Milk spilled off the side of the stairway.

Noory tried to grab onto the stairway railing to stop her fall. She tried to protect her belly as she somersaulted backwards down the stairs. Her head thudded against the steps, the back of her neck feeling the blow from the concrete edges.

She reached the sidewalk below. Noory grasped her belly and moaned.

A car pulled to the curb, the vehicle's headlights shining on Noory. A woman got out of the car and ran to Noory. She knelt down next to her.

"Are you okay?" she asked. "Oh, your head is bleeding."

"My belly hurts," said Noory.

"What's your name?"

"Noory."

"Hi, Noory. I'm Lila. Let's get you some help."

Lila dialed 911 on her phone.

"Okay. Help is on the way," she said.

The two apartment doors opened above them. Noory's mother saw her daughter's body framed in the headlights of the car at the curb.

"Oh, my Lord! Noory!" Nora Turner rushed down the stairs. "Baby! Are you okay? What happened?" Nora knelt down next to her daughter on the other side of Lila.

"I slipped on the stairs, Momma. My belly hurts." Noory touched her belly and winced.

Nora clasped her daughter's hand. "Oh, baby."

"Let me see if I can help you," said Lila. "Close your eyes. Okay, good. Now, try to breathe through the pain. Slowly. Breathe in and out. In and out. There you go. Good."

Lila stretched her fingers out above Noory's belly. She held her fingers taut as she slowly lowered them to Noory's stomach. Lila stroked Noory's belly lightly with her fingertips. She gently massaged her belly, then closed her own eyes and held her hands over Noory's stomach.

Lila took Nora's and Noory's hands in her own.

Static electricity popped between them.

"Don't worry," said Lila. "The baby will be fine."

An ambulance siren wailed in the distance.

At the hospital, Noory delivered a healthy baby boy. She named him Jamal.

~ 2 ~
Penns Grove, New Jersey

Jamal's father, Donald Williams, had never married Noory Turner. Donald had left New York for Florida when Jamal was only three years old, and Jamal's sister Janine only a year and half. Noory soon followed Donald to Florida, leaving Jamal and Janine with their grandmother in New York.

Donald returned north two years later and settled in Trenton, New Jersey. Donald invited Jamal to go on a canoe trip with him on the Delaware River to celebrate Jamal's fifth birthday.

Jamal and Donald set out on the river under the warm sunshine of an August afternoon. Donald showed Jamal how to paddle the canoe. Donald talked while they glided on the river.

"Jamal, you're five years old now. Pretty soon, you'll be a man. I want you to be a good man," said Donald. "I know I haven't been a good father to you and your sister. I never should have left Freeport. I was just a foolish young man."

The two paddled the boat to a small island in the river. They ate their lunch on the island. Jamal drank cherry soda and ate a peanut butter sandwich. His father ate a chicken sandwich and drank a beer.

Donald talked while they ate.

"Jamal, be someone who others can count on. I wasn't that man," said Donald, shaking his head."I didn't understand what it means to be a father. Or what it means to be a man. I made a lot of mistakes. We all make mistakes, Jamal. Now, I try to learn from my mistakes," said Donald. "I want you to learn from yours, too."

"Okay," said Jamal.

"Jamal, I wish I had lived my life differently," said Donald. "I didn't have a plan. You need to have a plan," he said.

"I made the mistake of dropping out of school when Noory got pregnant. That was a big mistake. Education can take you far in this world. Stay in school, Jamal. Maximize your future."

"What could I be?" asked Jamal.

"You can be anything you want to be."

"Anything?" said Jamal.

"Anything," said Donald. "The sky's the limit, Jamal."

"The sky's the limit," Jamal repeated.

"You'll have to work at it, and you'll have to pay your dues, but, if you set your mind to it, you can do anything," said Donald. "The most important thing is to just work hard and do good things. Everything else will fall into place."

Donald put his arm around Jamal.

"Happy Birthday, Jamal," said Donald. "You're five years old today. That's a big birthday."

Jamal smiled. It was his best birthday.

Donald and Jamal stayed too long on the river. The wind picked up in the late afternoon. The boat was whipped from side to side as they paddled against the current.

Donald tried to steer the boat close to shore. He paddled ferociously but the boat turned sideways in the current. The boat scraped against a rock and tipped over. Donald and Jamal were tossed into the water.

"Jamal, grab the boat!" yelled Donald.

Jamal held onto the corner of the capsized canoe.

Donald was pushed downstream. He bobbed up and down in the current.

"Jamal, hold on to the boat!" Donald yelled.

Jamal peered around the side of the canoe.

His father went under the water.

"Dad!" Jamal cried.

Donald surfaced. He bobbed up and down, moving farther away.

"Dad!" Jamal cried. "Come back! Dad! Come back!"

Donald went under the water again.

Jamal peered around the boat. His father didn't come back up.

"Dad!"

Jamal began to cry. The current pulled the boat away from him. Jamal thrashed and bobbed in the rough water. Like his father, Jamal went under.

Jamal's eyes opened at a snap of static electricity. A nurse held his wrist to take his pulse.

"Oh, I'm sorry about that," said the nurse. "It happens sometimes. Good morning. How do you feel?"

"Good morning," said Jamal, his voice raspy. "Thirsty."

The nurse lifted a straw to his lips. "Take a small sip." She placed the cup on the night stand. "Is that better?"

"Thank you," said Jamal. He lay back on the pillows in the hospital bed.

"How's your chest? Does it hurt to breathe?"

Jamal breathed in and out. "It hurts a little," he said.

"You swallowed a lot of water in the river," said the nurse. "Do you remember what happened?"

Jamal frowned. He nodded.

"My daddy went under the water."

"Yes. I'm very sorry," said the nurse. "Hikers found you on the river bank. Do you remember how you got there?"

Jamal shook his head.

"Well, that's okay," said the nurse. "I'm glad that you got to the bank. And I'm glad that you woke up on my shift so that I could meet you."

"It's nice to meet you, too," said Jamal.

The nurse smiled. She clasped Jamal's hands in her own. Static electricity again snapped between their palms.

Jamal pulled his hands back.

"I'm sorry," said the nurse. "That's twice, now. I guess that means that we're connected." The nurse smiled at him. "I'll let the doctor know that you're awake."

Jamal's grandmother sat on the green vinyl chair that was pulled alongside his hospital bed.

"Hi, Gran," said Jamal, his voice still raspy.

"Hello, Jamal," said his grandmother. "I've been waiting for you to wake up. How do you feel?"

"I'm a little tired."

"I guess you would be tired," said Nora. "It took a lot of energy to fight that current."

"It pushed me," said Jamal. "It pushed my daddy, too." He paused. "Gran, my daddy went under the water."

"I know, baby," said Nora. "I'm sorry. It's a tragedy about your daddy, Jamal."

"I went under the water, too," said Jamal.

"Yes, but somehow you made it to the river bank," said Nora. "That's a blessing."

"Gran, I saw an island under the water," said Jamal. "It had clear blue water and white sand and green palm trees. I started to swim to it."

"Under the water?" said Nora.

"Yes. But I heard my daddy calling to me. He told me not to swim to the island," said Jamal. "'The other way, the other way. Swim the other way,' he said."

Jamal sighed. "That's all I remember."

"Well, I guess your daddy was looking out for you that day," said Nora.

"I liked my daddy," said Jamal. "He showed me how to paddle the boat. He talked to me. He told me things."

"That's a wonderful memory for you to have, baby."

"My Daddy said that I could be whatever I wanted to be," said Jamal. "He told me to work hard and to do good things. The sky's the limit, he said."

"That's right, Jamal," said Nora. "You and Janine can be anything you want to be. The sky's the limit."

"Gran," said Jamal, "could you write down what my daddy told me so that I won't forget?"

"Yes, of course. Let me just find a pen and paper." Nora opened her purse. She took out a small notebook.

"Gran," said Jamal, "why was I saved but my daddy wasn't?"

"I don't know, Jamal," said Nora. "I truly don't. It's a tragedy that your daddy lost his life. It's a blessing that you survived," she said. "The Lord works in mysterious ways."

~ 3 ~
Freeport, New York

Jamal blew out the candles on his birthday cake.

"Happy Birthday!" said Jamal's sister, Janine.

"Happy Birthday," said his grandmother. "You're seventeen years old today," she said, shaking her head. "I still remember the day you were born, Jamal. It's stayed with me all these years."

Jamal and his sister smiled. His grandmother had told them the story of his birth at each one of Jamal's birthday celebrations.

"Mama fell down the steps and a woman put her hands on Mama's belly," said Janine. "Right?"

"That's right," said Nora. "Your mama fell down the steps and a lady named Lila pulled over to the curb to help. Lila lowered her palms to your mama's belly and held them there."

"She used her hands to heal Mama," said Janine.

"Yes, I think she did," said Nora. "When she was finished, she took our hands and held them in her own."

"Electricity," whispered Janine.

"Yes, that's right, baby. There was a spark of electricity in the lady's hands. That lady had a lot of energy in her hands.

She told us that the baby would be fine," said Nora.

"And the lady was right," said Nora. "Your Mama was taken to the hospital by ambulance and Jamal was born that same night, a healthy baby boy," said Nora.

"Happy 17th Birthday, Jamal!"

Jamal retrieved the small notebook from a wooden box underneath his bed. His grandmother had given it to him after he was released from the hospital when he was five years old. In the notebook, Nora had written down the advice that Jamal's father had imparted to him on the canoe trip.

Jamal read the pages each year on his birthday.

Be somebody that others can count on.
Learn from your mistakes.
Stay in school.
Maximize your future.
Work hard and do good things.
The sky's the limit.

Present Day

~ 1 ~

Delta Flight To Florida

Samantha Baker was the last stand-by passenger to board the Delta flight from New York to Fort Lauderdale.

"Please take any seat," said the flight attendant. "I'm afraid there are only middle seats left."

Samantha pulled her wheeled luggage down the aisle of the aircraft. She pulled it past the first two available rows. She stopped at the next available row.

The flight attendant located a bin for her bag.

Morgan Prince rose from his seat and stepped into the aisle of the aircraft to allow Samantha into the row.

Jamal Williams sat in the window seat. He glanced up and nodded at Samantha as she moved into the row. He glanced back down at his phone. His left earbud dangled over his chest.

The flight hit heavy turbulence as it neared Orlando. Passengers moaned as the plane was repeatedly lofted up and quickly dropped back down. The pilot's voice came over the intercom, his voice calm and smooth.

"Folks, I'm sorry about the rough ride. It seems that this storm is moving right along with us. So we're going to take a detour and wait out the storm on the ground at Palm Beach

Airport. I apologize for the delay and for any bumps ahead. We should be on the ground shortly. Thank you."

Samantha took the cup of club soda from the flight attendant and placed it on her tray. She intercepted a bottle of water from the attendant for her seat mate in the window seat.

"Thanks," he said.

"Hi. I'm Samantha."

"I'm Jamal."

"Are you listening to music?" Samantha asked.

"Yes."

"What kind of music do you like?" she asked.

"I like all kinds," said Jamal.

"Do you play an instrument?"

"No," said Jamal. "My mother played the piano but I don't seem to have her talent."

"Hmm," said Samantha. "I'd guess that you probably have another talent."

"Well, I like to take photographs," said Jamal.

"Ah, there you go," said Samantha. "Your mother has the ear. You have the eye. Are you a student?"

"Yes. I'm a junior in high school."

"I guess junior year comes with a lot of pressure," said Samantha. "Have you applied to colleges?"

"No. I'm not sure that I'm going to college," said Jamal.

"I'd encourage you to apply," said Samantha. "College can open a new world for you. It will give you opportunities to maximize your future," she said.

Jamal squinted at Samantha.

"Maximize your future," he repeated. "That's something my father once told me. It's weird hearing you say it."

"It's good advice," said Samantha. "Are you a good student?"

"I do okay."

"Are you on any school teams?" asked Samantha. "Do you perform any community service?"

"I'm on the football team at school," said Jamal. "My grandmother takes us to help out at a food pantry on the weekends."

"Jamal, I'm not an expert but it sounds to me like you have an excellent chance of acceptance to college," said Samantha. "You should talk to your guidance counselor."

Jamal nodded.

"Tell me," said Samantha, "why do you want to be a photographer?"

Jamal hesitated.

"I have a photograph of me sitting in a hospital bed when I was five years old," said Jamal. "In the picture, I look very small and very scared. When I see that photograph, it brings back everything I was feeling that day. I'd like to create that same emotion with my own photos."

"Ah, so you're an artist," said Samantha. "Then, you definitely should go to college. You must maximize your future."

Morgan Prince tapped his fingers against the screen of the device on his left wrist.

"Excuse me," said Samantha. "Is that a Smart Watch?"

"No," said Prince. "It's similar to a Smart Watch, but it's my firm's communication device. It has some proprietary features specific to my firm."

"That sounds important," said Samantha. "Can I ask what kind of work you do?"

"I'm a security agent. My job is protecting my firm's clients."

"That sounds like it could be dangerous."

"I suppose it can be, at times," said Prince, "but my firm provides excellent training. The firm prepares me for multiple scenarios on jobs. It makes it a little easier."

"It sounds like you enjoy it," said Samantha.

"I do. It can be exhilarating to save a life."

"I guess it would be. Hi. I'm Samantha," she said.

"Hi. I'm Morgan."

"Are you working now?" Samantha asked.

"Yes. I'm headed to an assignment in Hollywood."

"Will the flight delay affect your job?"

"Perhaps. Though, so far, it seems that it's still on," said Prince. "Are you also traveling for work, Samantha?"

"Yes. I'm headed to a monthlong house-sitting job in Fort Lauderdale."

"That's an interesting occupation," said Prince. "How did you get into that?"

"Dumb luck, really," said Samantha. "My mother recommended me to some friends of hers in New York City. The New York client recommended me to her sister in Florida."

"Do you think that you'll make it your career?"

"I doubt it," said Samantha, "but it works for me now. I'm looking forward to lounging at the pool in the Florida sunshine for a month."

"That sounds relaxing. Have you had other careers?"

"I spent my career in the accounting field," said Samantha. "I got a job right out of college for a firm in Charlotte. I went out on disability after a car accident," she said. "When I got back on my feet, I just never went back to accounting."

"Do you think you will?"

"At this point, probably not," said Samantha. "I think I'm looking for something different."

"Were you badly injured in the accident?"

"I was in a coma for five months," said Samantha. "My doctors called it a persistent vegetative state. They didn't expect me to wake up. The doctors told my mother, that if I did wake, I'd likely sustain significant brain damage," she said.

"But I woke up from the coma and I was fine," said Samantha. "My brain sustained no damage. I think that, when I was in the coma, I just experienced a different kind of consciousness." She paused.

"I guess that sounds weird," she said.

"No, it doesn't sound weird at all to me," said Prince. "I had a similar experience. My heart stopped while I was on the operating table," he said. "I heard the doctor call my death. But I wasn't dead," he said.

"Some call it near-death," Samantha whispered.

"Yes," said Prince. "I floated up out of my body and turned away from the panic in the operating room. I walked along a sandy path to the ocean. The sunset was phenomenal."

"I saw and heard so many strange and wonderful things while I was in the coma," said Samantha. "I just don't know if they're real, or if they're in the past, or in the future. I have had occasions when I get a sense that I've already experienced a situation or a conversation. I remember it from when I was in the coma. It's very strange and jarring," she said.

"I had a conversation with my stepfather when I was in the coma," said Samantha. "He gave me information to pass on to my mother. When I woke, I learned from my mother that my stepfather had died while I was in the coma," she said.

"But the information he gave me was accurate," said Samantha. "My mother found a missing key in the toe of my stepfather's slippers, just where he told me it would be." Samantha shook her head. "I think I was in some kind of a middle region."

"It was the strangest experience of my life," said Prince.

"What brought you back?" asked Samantha.

"I heard my daughter's voice calling me back. I floated back down into my body and my heart started to beat again. The doctors were shocked," he said. "What brought you out of your coma?" he asked.

"I saw my mother crying in the hospital bathroom after my doctors told her they had done everything they could for me," said Samantha. "And I heard my fiancé calling to me to wake up," said Samantha. "Unfortunately, when I did, he wasn't there. He died in the accident," she whispered.

"I'm sorry," said Prince.

"Thank you," said Samantha.

"It's interesting that we both heard loved ones calling us back," said Samantha. "Are you and your daughter close?"

"We were," said Prince. "Unfortunately, not now. I've lost contact with both of my girls."

"Oh. Why is that?" said Samantha.

"My wife got the girls in the divorce and took them across the country from California to New York. Our communication dwindled over time."

"Why?" asked Samantha.

"No good reason," said Prince. "As the girls grew older, it became increasingly awkward to communicate with them from a screen. My ex-wife remarried and the girls gained a doting stepfather."

"You're still their father," said Samantha.

"I know," said Prince. "I've been thinking about contacting them."

"It's never too late," said Samantha.

"Maybe I'll reach out," said Prince.

"I'm so amazed to meet you," he said. "You're the first person I've met who has shared the experience. It's hard to talk about with people who haven't experienced it."

"Yes," said Samantha. "It's not something that I typically discuss. People have a hard time understanding it. Sometimes, I even have a hard time wrapping my head around it," she said, "and I experienced it."

"Samantha, it's so amazing to meet you. I'd love to stay in touch, if you're okay with that," said Prince. "Would you be open to sharing contact information? I hope that's not too forward."

"Not at all, Morgan," said Samantha. "I'm also thrilled that we met. I'd like to stay in touch."

Samantha glanced at her seat mate in the window seat. He stared out the window of the plane. Both of his earbuds now dangled over his chest.

"Can you make it 'three for three'?" Samantha asked.

"Excuse me?" said Jamal.

"Can you make it three near-death survivors seated in the same row of an airplane?" Samantha said.

Jamal frowned.

"I'm kidding," said Samantha. "That would be something, though, wouldn't it?"

The pilot's voice came over the intercom.

"Good news, folks. The storm has cleared out of our path and we've been given clearance to continue to our destination. The flight attendants will come through the cabin to pick up any remaining trash," he said.

"Please buckle your seat belts. We'll be on our way shortly."

~ 2 ~
Hollywood, Florida

Prince sat at the counter of a twenty-four hour coffee shop in Hollywood, Florida. At 3:30 a.m., he was the only customer in the shop. The manager had delivered a cup of coffee to him and then disappeared into the back room.

Prince had spent the night patrolling the town but hadn't identified a client in need. He wondered if the flight delay had changed the job. He checked his wrist device. He had no new instructions.

Prince sipped his coffee. He stared up at the muted television behind the counter. He scratched a note on a napkin.

'Marie, I've been thinking a lot about the girls. Would it be possible for me to meet with them? May I call you a week from Friday for your response? I'll accept your answer, whatever it may be.'

Prince folded the napkin and placed it in the pocket of his jacket.

~ 3 ~

Fort Lauderdale Airport, Florida

"Happy Easter, Gran."

"Happy Easter, Jamal," said Nora. "Where are you calling from? It's very noisy."

"Oh, sorry about that," said Jamal. "Hold on a minute."

Jamal slung his bag over his shoulder and found an empty corner in the airport waiting room.

"Can you hear me better now, Gran?"

"Yes, now I can hear you, Jamal. Where are you?"

"At the airport. It's a little busy."

"You're at the airport this early?" said Nora. "Did you have breakfast with your mother this morning before church?"

"No. She left, Gran. When I got there for breakfast, she was gone."

"Oh, Jamal, I'm sorry," said Nora. "Did you have a good visit with her yesterday?"

"Yes," said Jamal. "We laughed a lot. She told me stories about when Janine and I were little."

"Good. That sounds like a nice visit."

"It was good, for a while," said Jamal. "But she started to fidget. I think that she ran out of stories to tell. I told her that

I'd see her for breakfast in the morning, and I left," said Jamal. "I think I freaked her out."

"Jamal, you did nothing wrong," said Nora. "Noory is my daughter and I love her, and I'll always love her. But I'm not blind to her faults. She's always had the bad habit of running away from uncomfortable situations."

"I don't want to be the reason she does drugs again," said Jamal.

"Jamal, it's not your fault," said his grandmother. "I suspect that Noory feels some level of guilt for running out on you and your sister. She silences that guilt with drugs. It's not your fault," she repeated.

Jamal sighed. "Okay," he said.

"What time will you get in?"

"Probably after eleven," said Jamal. "I'll take the train from JFK. Don't wait up."

"Should I leave dinner on the stove?"

"No, Gran, I'll eat something here before the flight."

"I'll leave you some dessert. Have a safe flight."

"Thanks, Gran."

~ 4 ~
Fort Lauderdale, Florida

Samantha called her mother.

"Happy Easter, Mom."

"Happy Easter, Samantha. It's nice to hear from you. How's the house?"

"It's beautiful," said Samantha. "I'm having coffee outside by the pool. The garden is gorgeous."

"It sounds like you could get spoiled."

"I think I could," said Samantha.

"How was your flight down?"

"The turbulence was awful," said Samantha. "Our flight was diverted to Palm Beach to wait out a storm."

"Well, I'm glad you made it there safely," said Peggy.

"I had a bit of an odd encounter on the plane," said Samantha. "My seat mate told me that he heard the doctors call his death after his heart failed," said Samantha. "But he survived. Like me."

"Samantha, that's an interesting conversation to have on an airplane with a stranger," said Peggy.

"I guess I brought it up," said Samantha.

"Hmm," said Peggy.

"Mom, it was amazing to meet someone else who's shared the experience," said Samantha. "We exchanged contact information. I think that I can learn from him."

"What is it that you want to learn, Samantha?"

"How best to live my life, knowing that I've been saved," said Samantha.

Samantha typed a message to the contact number Prince had given her on the airplane.

'Hi, Morgan. I enjoyed our conversation on the plane. I hope our schedules align so that we can meet again soon.'

Morgan responded quickly.

'I look forward to it. I hope you are enjoying the Florida sunshine.'

~ 5 ~
Freeport, New York

Jamal entered his grandmother's apartment at half past eleven on Easter night. He stored his bag in his bedroom and visited the kitchen. His grandmother had left him a slice of apple pie on the counter. She had left a note on top of the cellophane wrap that covered the pie.

Happy Easter.

Jamal poured a glass of milk and sat down at the table.

Jamal's grandmother called to him from the end of the hallway. "Jamal, is that you?"

"Yes, it's me, Gran. I'm sorry if I woke you."

"No, no. It's okay. I was half-listening in my sleep."

Nora entered the kitchen. "How's the pie?"

"It's good, Gran. Thanks."

Nora sat across from Jamal at the table.

"I'm sorry that your visit with your mother didn't go better. How are you feeling?"

"I'm okay," said Jamal. "I'm just disappointed."

"I can understand that," said Nora. "My daughter has disappointed me a time or two."

Jamal frowned.

"Gran, Mama said that I was marked as special when I was born," said Jamal. "She said that's why I survived the canoe accident when I was five."

"You are special, Jamal. Your mama's right."

"Not like that, Gran. On the plane down to Florida, both of my seat mates said that they had died and come back. They called themselves near-death survivors," said Jamal. "Gran, is that what I am?"

"Jamal, I don't understand," said his grandmother.

"Neither do I," said Jamal, shaking his head.

Nora squinted at him.

"The man in the aisle seat said he heard the doctors call his death when he was on the operating table. He said that he came back when he heard his daughter's voice calling him," said Jamal.

"The lady in the seat next to me said that she experienced a different level of consciousness when she was in a coma. She said that she talked to a dead man. She said that she woke from the coma when she heard her fiancé calling her back."

"Jamal, what does that have to do with you?" said Nora.

"It's made me think about what happened to me," said Jamal. "Gran, when I was born, that lady, Lila, helped Mama. And when I went under the water after the canoe accident, I heard my daddy's voice telling me not to swim to the island under the water. Somehow, I survived my mama's fall and the canoe accident."

"You were blessed," said Nora.

"I've been thinking that maybe I'm like my seat mates," said Jamal. "I drowned, like my daddy did, but I came back. Gran, why was I saved?"

"Jamal, I guess there are some things in this world that we're not meant to understand," said Nora. "Just accept the blessing."

~ 6 ~
La Jolla, California

"Hi, Marie. Is now still a good time to talk?"

"Hello, Morgan. Yes, now is fine," said Marie. "Thank you for sending your note. It gave us all some time to think it through."

"Marie, I know it's an awkward situation," said Morgan. "I regret that I lost touch with the girls. I'd just like to get to know them again, if that's possible. I'll accept whatever the answer is, yes or no."

"Well, it's mixed," said Marie. "Alicia has agreed to meet with you. Gwen hasn't."

"Okay. I accept that," said Morgan. "I would love to meet with Alicia."

"Would you like to schedule something now?"

"Hmm, my work schedule is fairly unpredictable," said Morgan. "I'm still traveling a lot for my job. May I contact you when I'll be in the New York City area?"

"Well, okay," said Marie, "but the more advance notice you can give us, the better. Alicia has a lot of after-school activities. She may not be able to meet on short notice."

"I understand. I'll keep trying," said Morgan. "I hope

that, one day, our schedules will align enough for us to have a quick cup of tea, or, even, to chat on a park bench for a few minutes. Whatever works best on such short notice."

"Okay, Morgan, we'll wing it," said Marie. "Contact me when you're available, and I'll check Alicia's schedule."

"Thanks, Marie."

"Morgan, they're your daughters, too," said Marie. "Dan and I would both like for you to be in their lives."

~ 7 ~
Charlotte, North Carolina

Samantha returned home to Charlotte after her house-sitting job ended in Fort Lauderdale. She called her mother.

"Hi, Mom," said Samantha. "What are you doing?"

"I'm having a cup of tea on the terrace before I leave for a book club meeting," said Peggy.

"You joined a book club? What are you reading?"

"Oh, I just joined the group," said Peggy. "I'm just going tonight to listen to them discuss the book they've been reading."

"I see," said Samantha.

"I guess you'll miss Fort Lauderdale," said Peggy. "It sounds like it was beautiful."

"It was," said Samantha. "It was a wonderful break. It gave me a lot of time to think."

"What have you been thinking, Samantha?"

"I've been thinking that it's okay to grieve Kip's loss but I need to move forward. I need to learn to live without him."

"Yes," said Peggy. "It's not easy but it's the only thing that we can do. Hence, the book club."

"Mom, I wanted to ask you something."

"Yes?"

"I've been thinking about sending a note to Kip's parents. What do you think about that?"

"I think it's a wonderful idea, Samantha."

Samantha reread her note to Kip's family.

'Dear Lynn, Felix, and Lydia,

Please accept my belated condolences on Kip's passing. May I express my condolences to you in person?

Thank you.'

A reply note arrived the following week.

'Dear Samantha,

Thank you for your condolences.

Are you available for four o'clock tea on the 19th?

Lynn, Felix, and Lydia'

Samantha parked in front of the small brick house in the neighborhood west of Uptown Charlotte. She sat with her hands on the car's steering wheel and stared out the passenger window at Kip's parents' house.

A curtain moved across the front window.

Kip's mother, Lynn, stepped outside the front door.

Samantha took a deep breath. She opened the car door.

Samantha walked to the curb at the end of the driveway. She blinked away tears as she walked up the driveway to meet Kip's mother.

"Hello, Samantha. It's good to see you," said Lynn.

"Hello, Mrs. Fields. Thank you for inviting me."

"Felix and Lydia are waiting for us in the den."

Lynn ushered Samantha into the house.

Kip's sister, Lydia, rose from the couch when Samantha entered the room. Lydia hugged her. "We missed you," she whispered.

Kip's father, Felix, stood up from the wing chair next to the fireplace. "Hello, Samantha. It's good to see you," he said.

"Hello, Mr. Fields. Thank you for your invitation."

"Samantha you can sit on the couch next to Lydia," said Lynn Fields. "Lydia, will you pour the tea?"

Samantha sipped her tea. "That has a nice flavor," she said. "What's the variety?"

"It's oolong," said Lydia. She smiled. "I'm glad that you like it."

"We had so many nice afternoons here over tea," said Samantha. She glanced down to hide the tears in her eyes. "I'm so sorry about Kip," she whispered.

"Thank you, Samantha," said Lynn.

"I'm so sorry that he's gone," said Samantha.

"Yes, we all are," said Lynn.

"I'm sorry for being so selfish in my own grief that I didn't acknowledge yours," said Samantha. "I'm sorry for sending Kip's belongings here without notifying you. That was cruel. I'm very sorry," said Samantha. She wiped at the tears that rolled down her cheeks.

"Thank you, Samantha," said Lynn.

"You must miss him terribly."

"Yes, of course, we do," said Lynn. "We miss him every single day. But not only did we lose our son but we lost our future daughter-in-law. You just dropped out of our lives."

"I know. I'm sorry. I just couldn't face you," said Samantha. "I couldn't see how you could ever forgive me for Kip's death."

"Samantha," said Lynn, "Kip's death was tragic but you

are not to blame."

"I made him leave the party that night," said Samantha, in a whisper. "We argued about it. If we had only stayed overnight," she said. "I just keep thinking that if I hadn't made him leave the party, he'd still be with us."

"Samantha," said Felix, sharply, "it was an accident. The driver of the other vehicle was drunk on New Year's Eve and he ran his red light. It's not your fault,"he said.

"As Lynn said, Kip's death was a tragedy for this family," said Felix. "And this family includes you, Samantha. You'll always be a member of this family."

Samantha waited on the front stoop of her duplex apartment for her neighbor Rosa to return from work.

"When is she coming?" asked Carla, Rosa's daughter.

"She should be here soon," said Samantha.

"We just have to wait," said Carla's brother Johnny.

Carla stepped off the stoop. She stared across the apartment complex for a sign of her mother's arrival home.

"Samantha, were you ever in a fight?" Johnny asked.

"No, I don't think I ever was," said Samantha. "Why? Were you?"

"Not yet," said Johnny. "But I might be."

"Why?"

"Jimmy Smith says I'm chicken because I won't play dodgeball at recess."

"Why won't you play?" asked Samantha.

"Because Jimmy aims for me," said Johnny. "It hurts when he hits me."

"That's why they call it dodge ball," said Samantha. "You have to learn to jump out of the way."

"I know how to do it," said Carla. "Like this." She

hopped from side to side on the sidewalk.

"I think Jimmy wants to fight about it," said Johnny.

"Then, you do this." Carla put up her fists and jabbed forward on her toes.

"That's not how you do it," said Johnny. He sighed. "Maybe I'll just play dodgeball and let him hit me."

"Maybe you'll get better and he won't hit you as often," said Samantha.

"I see her! I see her!" yelled Carla.

The children raced across the apartment complex to escort their mother home.

Samantha sat at Rosa's kitchen table after the children were in bed for the night.

"Samantha, thank you for watching the kids tonight," said Rosa. "Overtime doesn't come around too often anymore. Thank you for allowing me to take advantage of it."

"You're welcome, Rosa," said Samantha. "I had no plans tonight. And, you know I love spending time with your kids."

"Thank you," said Rosa.

They sipped their wine.

"How was the house-sitting job in Florida?" Rosa asked.

"It was a heavenly vacation," said Samantha. "The house was beautiful. It had a patio and a pool with a gorgeous garden surrounding it. I drank my coffee out there in the mornings and had a glass of wine out there in the evenings."

"That does sound heavenly," said Rosa. "How fun to slip into someone else's home and live their life for a short period of time."

"It was fun," said Samantha. "And it gave me time to think."

"That sounds deep," said Rosa.

"I've been struggling with grief over losing Kip," said Samantha. "While I've regained my physical strength, my grief has debilitated me. I've just been drifting along."

"Everyone grieves in their own time," said Rosa. "You lost your fiancé," she said. "It's understandable."

"What I realized in Florida," said Samantha, "is that grieving Kip's loss doesn't have to mean that I forgo my own life. I've been given a precious gift. I survived."

"Yes. You were blessed," said Rosa.

"I feel like I need to make myself worthy of being blessed," said Samantha. She squinted at Rosa. "Have you ever heard of near-death?"

Rosa made the sign of the cross.

"My seat mate on the plane to Florida told me that he was a near-death survivor," said Samantha. "He said that his heart failed and his doctor called his death."

Rosa's eyes narrowed.

"He said that he went back into his body when he heard his daughter calling to him. He said that his heart started to beat again," said Samantha. "What do you think about that?"

"Love brought him back," whispered Rosa.

"But, why, do you think?"

"He must have unfinished business," said Rosa.

"Hmm," said Samantha. "Maybe."

Samantha stood from the table. "Rosa, thank you for the lovely evening. Johnny and Carla can come up to my place for breakfast, if you want to sleep in."

"Thank you. I'm looking forward to sleeping in. I already told Johnny to get cereal for breakfast and watch television until I get up," said Rosa.

"Enjoy," said Samantha.

~ 8 ~
Freeport, New York

Jamal knocked on his guidance counselor's open door.

"Mr. Martin, do you have a few minutes?"

"Come in, Jamal. How can I help you?"

"Can I talk to you about college?"

"Sure," said Mr. Martin. "Have a seat."

Jamal placed his backpack on the floor. He sat in the chair in front of Martin's desk.

Mr. Martin turned his chair to his computer. He typed on his keyboard. He reviewed Jamal's record on the screen,

"You're a good candidate, Jamal. I would definitely encourage you to apply to college."

"What if I can't afford to pay for it?" said Jamal.

"Let's not worry about that yet," said Mr. Martin. "The first step is to gain acceptance. When that happens, I can help you to apply for the whole gamut of financial assistance."

"What's the process?" asked Jamal.

"You'll fill out a universal application that will get sent to each of the schools to which you apply," said Mr. Martin. "Each application requires a fee. Is that a problem?"

"I work. I can save up for it," said Jamal.

"Okay. Good. Can I recommend a strategy?" said Mr. Martin. "I'd recommend that you apply to five schools, choosing each one to maximize the probability of acceptance to at least one school."

"Which schools?" said Jamal.

"I'd suggest that you apply to two state schools," said Mr. Martin. "Tuition is free if you meet the state's income threshold. You could even live at home to save money on room and board."

"That sounds good," said Jamal.

"Next, I'd recommend that you apply to a community college, like Nassau," said Mr. Martin. "You can pick up credits there and transfer to another school for your last two years."

"Okay," said Jamal.

"That leaves two reach schools."

"What are reach schools?" asked Jamal.

"Schools with very good credentials that are very hard to get into," said Mr. Martin.

"You mean schools that I have very little chance of getting into," said Jamal.

"Jamal, don't sell yourself short," said Mr. Martin. "If you could choose any school to attend, which would it be?"

"NYU. For photography."

"Well, let's put it on the list," said Mr. Martin. "That leaves one more reach school."

Jamal shrugged.

"Okay, we can figure that out later," said Mr. Martin. He swiveled his chair back to his computer and pulled up the admissions information for NYU. Martin scanned the requirements. He printed a copy for Jamal.

"The visual arts program requires that you submit a portfolio of your work," he said. "You'll need to submit a collection of photographs to showcase your talent and passion for the work."

"Okay," said Jamal.

"You'll also have to write an essay," said Mr. Martin.

"Is there a theme?" asked Jamal.

"No," said Martin. "The purpose of the essay is to help the admissions committee understand who you are and why you think their school is a good fit for you," said Mr. Martin. "The essay can help you to stand out in a crowd of qualified applicants."

Jamal scribbled in his notebook at the break room table in the Freeport Stop and Shop.

His coworker Vanessa entered the room and took a seat across from him at the table. She shook a bottle of chocolate milk.

"Hi, Jamal," said Vanessa. "What are you doing?"

"I'm working on my college essay."

"You're going to college?"

"I'm applying. An essay is required with the application."

"What's it about?" said Vanessa.

"I'm writing about something that happened when I was five years old," said Jamal.

"Read it to me," said Vanessa.

"It's just a first draft," said Jamal.

He read from his notebook.

"There is a photograph of me when I was five years old. I was sitting in a hospital bed after a canoe accident that resulted in the death of my father. The canoe trip was the first time I had seen my father in almost three years and the last time I ever saw him.

"The photograph of me in the hospital bed captures the shock, the pain, and the grief of that terrible day. That photograph is why I'm a photographer today."

~ 9 ~

Astor Coffeehouse, New York City

Morgan Prince stood from his table when his ex-wife entered the Astor Coffeehouse. Dan and Prince's younger daughter, Alicia, followed Marie.

"Hello, Morgan," said Marie. "You're looking well."

"Hi, Marie. Thank you. I'm feeling well," said Prince. "You're also looking well. Thank you for setting this up."

Morgan shook hands with Dan. He smiled at Alicia.

"Thank you for agreeing to meet with me, Alicia."

"You're welcome."

Prince smiled.

"Alicia, are you okay here?" asked Marie.

"Yes, Mom, I'm fine."

"Okay. I'll see you later, honey. Goodbye, Morgan."

"Can I call you Morgan?" Alicia asked.

"Yes," said Morgan. "That would be fine."

"Okay. Good." Alicia sipped her hot chocolate.

"So, where shall we start?" said Morgan.

"In school, we do ice breakers," said Alicia.

"You start."

"Where did you eat breakfast this morning?"

"In a diner in New Milford, New Jersey."

"Why were you there?" asked Alicia.

"For work."

"Are you a security agent?" said Alicia.

"Yes. I travel a lot for my job."

"Okay, your turn," said Alicia.

"What is your most favorite possession?"

"My violin."

"Do you take lessons?" asked Morgan.

"Yes. And I'm in the school band."

"Do you wear a uniform to school?" asked Morgan.

"Yes. It's plaid. I'm a freak on the subway."

Morgan smiled. "Do you play any sports?"

"Ice hockey."

"You play the violin and you play ice hockey?"

"Gwen says ice hockey unleashes my inner monster," said Alicia. She shrugged. "I just think it's fun."

"How long have you been playing?" Morgan asked.

"Three years," said Alicia. "My mom posts pictures of my games sometimes. She going to post pictures of Gwen in her prom dress."

"Do you and Gwen go to the same school?"

"No. Gwen goes to school downtown. I go to a school uptown."

"How do you get there?"

"Mostly, my Mom drives me," said Alicia. "But sometimes, I take the subway home."

"What subway line do you take?"

"I take the six to Grand Central and then take the shuttle to Times Square and take the 1 Train home. Sometimes, I stay on the six."

"Wow, I guess I'm not the only one who travels," said Morgan.

"Do you live in La Jolla?" asked Alicia.

"Yes," said Morgan. "I sold the house in San Diego a few years ago. I live in a condo in La Jolla now."

"Gwen says La Jolla is posh."

Morgan chuckled.

"Remember when Gwen and I came out for the summer?" said Alicia. "That was fun. Even Gwen had fun."

"Do you and Gwen get along?" Morgan asked.

"Mostly," said Alicia. "She gets mad at me a lot but she gets over it."

"I suppose you get mad at her, too," said Morgan.

Alicia nodded. "But I get over it."

"It sounds like you're normal sisters," said Morgan.

Alicia squinted at Morgan. "Are you dying?"

"No," said Morgan. "I'm not dying. Why would you think that?"

"Gwen thinks that's why you reached out to us."

Morgan frowned. "I can understand why she'd say that. It's been a while since we've had contact," he said. He shook his head.

"The only reason I contacted your mother was that I wanted to reestablish contact with you and your sister. I made such a mistake, letting you go. My only goal is to get to know you both again."

Alicia nodded. "Okay." She sipped her tea.

"Do you have any pets?" asked Alicia.

"No," said Morgan. "I travel too frequently to properly care for a pet. Do you?"

"Yes, we have a chihuahua named Frank."

"It's a good name," said Morgan.

Alicia smiled.

~ 10 ~
Charlotte, North Carolina

Samantha walked five dogs in Freedom Park on a gusty summer day. The wind lifted the baseball cap from her head and lofted it down the slope to the lake. Samantha pulled the dogs down the slope to retrieve it.

A man dressed in a light gray business suit with a melon-colored tie stood at the edge of the lake. He deftly put his foot down on the cap before it reached the water. He picked up the hat and dusted it off as Samantha approached with the dogs.

"Is this yours?" he asked.

The dogs barked at him.

"Hey!" said Samantha. "Behave!"

"Yes. Thank you." She took the cap from the man. She pulled it tightly over her head.

The dogs barked excitedly. They circled Samantha and the man, their leashes becoming entangled.

"I'm sorry," said Samantha. "This is a big change in their routine. Katja!" she called. "Come here now!"

The black and white Akita wound his leash back around and stood alongside Samantha. She patted the dog's head. "Good boy." She tightened his leash.

"Harold!" she called to the Great Dane. "Over here! Now!"

The Great Dane joined Katja at Samantha's side.

"Well, that's two," said Samantha. "They can be a handful." She unraveled the leashes of the three remaining dogs.

"Okay," she said. "Thank you for saving my hat."

"It was my pleasure," said the man. "I wonder, though. Could we have a conversation?"

"Excuse me?" said Samantha. "I have to walk the dogs."

"Just a conversation," said the man. "I'll join you on your walk. I'll even take a dog or two off your hands." The man followed behind Samantha as she pulled the dogs up the slope to the walkway. "May I walk with you for a bit?" he asked.

Samantha glanced around at her surroundings. Groups of people strolled in both directions on the sidewalk.

"I mean no harm," he said.

"Okay," said Samantha. She handed him the leashes for Harold and Katja.

"I'm David Bromwell."

"Hello. I'm Samantha Baker."

"It's nice to meet you, Samantha."

"You look like you should be in a business meeting," said Samantha.

"As I was this morning." Mr. Bromwell smiled.

"Do you live in Charlotte?" Samantha asked.

"No. I'm here interviewing candidates for an open position that's based here. My admin Krista suggested that I take the afternoon off and visit this park. It was an excellent suggestion."

"It's a beautiful day," said Samantha.

"Is Charlotte your home?" he asked.

"Yes," said Samantha.

"Is walking dogs your career?" Mr. Bromwell asked.

"My career?" said Samantha. "No. I don't think so. It works for now, though."

"Would you accept a job if the right opportunity came along?"

"Maybe. Probably. I'm just not sure what that might be," said Samantha.

"Perhaps you should apply for my open position," said Mr. Bromwell. "I think it might suit you well."

"Doing what?" said Samantha

Mr. Bromwell pulled a business card from his suit pocket. "I manage a team at Ascenda Security," he said. "The firm deploys talent and technology to achieve success in our industry."

"And why do you think I would be good at it?"

"You managed the unexpected situation with the dogs very competently," said Mr. Bromwell.

"Untangling their leashes?"

"My agents run into unforeseen circumstances quite frequently," said Mr. Bromwell. "Being able to handle chaos is no small thing. It's an excellent quality in an agent."

"I recently met someone who worked as a security agent. He liked it," said Samantha.

"It can be exhilarating to save a life."

"That's exactly what he said."

"Well, don't you think it would be exhilarating to save a life?" asked Mr. Bromwell.

"Well, yes. Sure. Of course," said Samantha.

Mr. Bromwell stopped on the sidewalk. He handed the leashes for Katja and Harold back to Samantha.

"I'll leave you now, Ms. Baker. If you're interested in exploring the position further, please call the number on the back of my card. My assistant Krista will set things up. It's been a pleasure meeting you. Thank you for the conversation."

Samantha took the elevator to the top floor of a sleek office building in Uptown Charlotte. She stepped out of the elevator into the lounge of a modern office suite. The decor was all-white, with floor-to-ceiling glass walls on two sides. The lounge was furnished with white couches and arm chairs. A video screen ran clips of employees from around the world.

Samantha approached the woman sitting behind the large glossy white desk in the center of the room. A gate behind the desk led to several rows of empty white workstations.

"Good morning. I'm Samantha Baker. Are you Krista?"

"Yes, I am." Krista smiled. "Good morning, Samantha. Did you have any trouble finding us?"

"No. Your directions were excellent," said Samantha. "Thank you."

"Why don't you have a seat in the lounge?" said Krista. "I expect Mr. Bromwell shortly."

Samantha sat in a white arm chair and watched the employee videos.

"Ms. Baker?" Krista called.

"I'm very sorry," said Krista, as Samantha approached the reception desk.

"Mr. Bromwell won't be able to meet with you, after all. He was called out for an emergency this morning. I'm sorry."

"I see," said Samantha, nodding. "Okay. Well, it seemed to be too good to be true, anyway. Thank you for your help, Krista. Enjoy your day." Samantha turned to go.

"Oh, no, Ms. Baker. Please, wait," said Krista. "Mr. Bromwell apologized for not keeping his appointment with you but he asked me to get the papers together."

"The papers?" said Samantha.

"Mr. Bromwell is offering you a position with the firm."

"He's offering me a job without a formal interview?"

"Yes. That's how it happens, sometimes," said Krista.

"Mr. Bromwell says that he has a feel for these things." She handed a stack of documents to Samantha.

"Please read each of the documents carefully," said Krista. "If everything looks in order, please sign where noted and return to me."

"I'm feeling a little overwhelmed," said Samantha. "This is so unexpected. Would you mind if I took a desk and reviewed the documents here?"

"That's no problem at all," said Krista. She opened the gate behind her and led Samantha to the area housing the workstations.

"Why are all the desks empty?" asked Samantha.

"They're a convenience for employees should they need to use them in their travels," said Krista. "Most days, I'm here by myself. I hardly even notice them anymore." She chuckled.

"Have you worked for Mr. Bromwell for very long?"

"Oh, yes, quite a while," said Krista. "I think we make a good team."

Samantha sat at a white workstation to read through the documents. The top document in the stack was the firm's offer of employment. The second document specified that company-issued communication devices could only be used for company business. Samantha read through the remaining documents.

Samantha reread the complete set of documents. She signed each document where required. She returned the documents to Krista.

"Welcome aboard, Samantha," said Krista.

~ 11 ~
Santa Barbara, California

Samantha rang the doorbell of her mother's home in Santa Barbara. She rang the bell again and waited. She found her mother's house key on her key ring and opened the door. She stepped inside the house.

"Hello!" she called. "Mom, are you here? Mom?" she called. "It's Samantha. Are you here?"

"Samantha?" Peggy appeared at the top of the stairs in a white bathrobe, with a white turban around her hair.

"I thought I heard the bell," said Peggy. "What a surprise to find you at my door, Samantha."

"I'm sorry that my visit is so last-minute," said Samantha. "I had a training class for a new job in Santa Monica. The class ended earlier than I expected so I came here. Is that okay? Am I disturbing you?"

"Don't be silly, Samantha. I'm glad you're here. I was just getting ready for dinner in town with my friend Harold. Would you like to join us?"

"No. Thank you, Mom," said Samantha. "You go. I think I'd like to stay here and listen to the birds, if that's okay."

"Yes, of course," said Peggy. "Okay, well I'm going to

get dressed now. You know where everything is. Make yourself comfortable. I'll be down shortly."

Peggy joined Samantha on the terrace, dressed for her dinner date.

"Samantha, I'm heading out now. I should be back by ten, I think," said Peggy.

"You look nice, Mom."

"Thank you," said Peggy. "You look healthy, Samantha. Fit," she said.

"I am, Mom. I've had a lot of physical training for a new job as a security agent. I just came from a session on Tai Chi on the beach in Santa Monica."

"Tai Chi," repeated Peggy. "Yes, I've heard of it. Have you heard of Qi Dong?"

"Yes, I've heard of it," said Samantha, "but I haven't been trained in it. Do you practice it, Mom?"

"Me? Oh, no. I'm too busy for that," said Peggy. "It's all the rage at the club, though."

Samantha smiled.

"So, no more dog walking?" Peggy asked.

"No more dog walking, no more house-sitting," said Samantha. "It feels like the right thing for me."

"Well, good for you," said Peggy. "It sounds like you're moving forward."

"I guess we both are, Mom," said Samantha.

Peggy carried a tea tray out to the terrace.

"Hi, Mom," said Samantha. "How was your date?"

"Very nice. I always enjoy Harold's company. "

"Do I know Harold?" asked Samantha.

"He's a new friend from my book club," said Peggy.

"So, the book club is working out?" said Samantha.

"Yes," said Peggy. "I've made a few friends. It gets me out of the house," she said. "How was your evening, Samantha?"

"Relaxing," said Samantha. "I love it here."

"I do, too. You know that you're always welcome, Samantha."

"Mom, I was remembering what you said to me when I was in the coma. You apologized for moving me around so much. Too many memories, you said."

Peggy nodded.

"But you're staying here. Without Stanley."

"I am staying," said Peggy. "I miss Stanley terribly. He was so interesting. Life is quite boring without him. And every memory reminds me that he's gone. But it feels like the right thing to stay here."

Samantha nodded.

"Mom, I feel so much better since I resolved the situation with Kip's family."

"Bravo, Samantha. I'm proud of you," said Peggy. She shook her head. "I blame myself, you know," she said.

"I knew it was a mistake to let you go back to Charlotte alone," said Peggy. "It was too soon. I should have gone back with you. I think that I could have helped you. With Kip's things, for instance."

"It wasn't my finest hour," said Samantha.

"Grief is a powerful emotion," said Peggy.

~ 12 ~
Las Vegas, Nevada

Morgan Prince called out to the man who climbed above him on the New York New York Hotel roller coaster on the Las Vegas Strip.

The man climbed three more rungs of the coaster. He stopped and stared down at Prince.

"Go back, sir," he said. "This isn't your business."

"What's your name?"

The man climbed another rung.

"Edgar."

"Hi, Edgar. I'm Morgan. Why are you up here?"

"I lost my job yesterday," said Edgar. "I can't provide for my family. I couldn't tell my wife," he said. "I left home this morning for work as I usually do, but I had no place to go."

"Edgar, you're just going through a rough patch," said Prince. "Things will get better."

"How do you know?" said Edgar.

"Because your family loves you," said Prince. "They'll support you through tough times. You need to trust in their love."

"I can't provide for them," said Edgar.

"Do you have children?" asked Prince.

"Yes, I have two girls, six and eight."

"I also have two girls," said Prince, "but they're teenagers now. Children grow up so fast. Your girls need you, Edgar. They love you. Don't give that up."

Edgar stared down at Prince.

"I'm speaking from experience," said Prince. "I let my girls go some time back. I lost all communication with them. Now, I'm back in contact with them. My girls bring me joy, no matter what the circumstances of my life. Your daughters can bring you joy even in the rough times."

Edgar stared down at Prince.

A crowd had gathered across the street on Las Vegas Boulevard. People held up their phones, recording the scene.

Prince glanced up at Edgar.

"That crowd over there is only going to get larger, Edgar. The news media will be here soon. Let me take you into the hotel. I can call in some folks to help you. We can call your family. Please let me help you," said Prince. "Things will work out."

Edgar stared at the noisy crowd across the street. He glanced up to the top of the roller coaster.

"Okay," he said.

"Follow me down," said Prince.

The two climbed back down the coaster and dropped to the hotel's roof.

Prince waved his wrist device in front of a fire door. He used his device to unlock the room closest to the fire door.

"Okay, first, let me contact a few people who can help you," said Prince. He tapped a message on his device.

"Help is on the way," said Prince. "Now, let's call your family."

Morgan Prince sipped coffee in a yellow leather arm chair in the lounge of the Bellagio Hotel. He watched the television mounted on the wall of the lounge.

A reporter stood in front of the New York New York Hotel.

"A Good Samaritan talked a would-be suicide jumper down from the iconic roller coaster atop the New York New York Hotel this afternoon. Neither man has been identified by the police," said the reporter. "The investigation continues."

Prince stood from the arm chair. He left the Bellagio. Prince walked down the long driveway leading out to Las Vegas Boulevard.

Samantha sat at the nearly empty bar in Harrah's Casino. Despite an availability of open seats, she watched as a man took the bar stool next to an older woman who was alone.

The man ordered a drink for himself.

He flashed a smile at the older woman seated next to him. He engaged the woman in conversation. He bought the woman a drink.

Samantha rose from her seat.

She moved behind the couple at the bar.

As the man chatted with the older woman, he deftly lifted her purse from the back of her chair.

Samantha stepped up and grabbed the purse.

"I believe this belongs to the lady," said Samantha.

The man let go of the purse.

Samantha flagged the bartender. "This guy just tried to lift this woman's purse."

"Time to move on," said the bartender. He reached for the man's drink.

"I paid for that drink and I'm damn well going to drink

it," said the man. He downed the drink and slapped the glass down on the bar. The security guard escorted him out of the casino.

Samantha returned the purse to the woman at the bar. "Are you okay?" she asked.

"Yes, I'm fine," said the woman. "Thank you."

"Hi. I'm Samantha Baker."

"Hello. I'm Ida Parker. He seemed like such a nice man."

"Yes. And that's how he was going to rob you," said Samantha. "Never leave your purse out of your sight."

"Oh, I was foolish to come here alone," said Ida. "This was my late husband Frank's favorite bar in Vegas. I guess I was just trying to recapture the good times we had here."

"I'm very sorry for your loss, Ida," said Samantha. "You must miss him."

"I do. We were married for fifty-eight years," said Ida. "I'm still not used to living without him."

"I can understand that," said Samantha. "I also lost someone close to me," she said. "It's not easy to move forward alone."

"I guess I haven't adjusted to it," said Ida.

"They say it takes time," said Samantha.

"That's what they say," said Ida. "Well, thank you for helping me tonight. I suppose I should just go back to my hotel and wait for my friends to come back from their show."

"Would you allow me to escort you?" said Samantha.

Ida's phone rang as the taxi cab pulled into the long driveway of the Bellagio Hotel.

"I'm coming up the driveway now," said Ida.

"My friends are waiting for me in the lobby," she told Samantha. "We're going out for dessert."

"That sounds like fun," said Samantha.

"Would you like to join us?"

"Thank you for asking," said Samantha, "but I still have to do a bit of work this evening. Enjoy the night with your friends."

Samantha escorted Ida into the hotel lobby. Ida's friends rose to greet her.

"Will you be okay now, Ida?" said Samantha.

"Yes. Thank you for watching out for a foolish old woman tonight."

Samantha walked down the driveway of the Bellagio Hotel to Las Vegas Boulevard.

Samantha sipped a glass of wine in the Chandelier Bar in the Las Vegas Cosmopolitan Hotel. She typed a message to Morgan.

'Were you at the New York New York roller coaster today? Are you still here? I'm at the Chandelier Bar.'

Samantha prepared her daily report for the firm, detailing the results of the evening's training task. She submitted her report and closed up her tablet. She stowed it in her briefcase on the floor next to her chair. She relaxed in the luxury of the room.

"Samantha?"

"Morgan Prince!" said Samantha. "Hi. You got my text?"

"Yes. Hi. It's good to see you, Samantha. May I join you?"

"Yes, of course," said Samantha.

Prince placed his drink on the table between their chairs. "What a surprise that we're both here."

"So, were you the good Samaritan? Were you working?"

"Yes," said Prince. "Why are you here?"

"I'm working, too," said Samantha. "I have a new job.

I'm here in Las Vegas for a training session."

"Congratulations. What kind of work?"

"I have a job with a security company."

"No more house-sitting?"

"No. I gave up all my odd jobs," said Samantha. "I'm working full-time now."

"Wow, that's different," said Prince. "Which firm do you work for?"

Samantha reached down to her briefcase and held up the laminated tag that hung from its strap.

"Ascenda Security," she said.

Prince squinted at the familiar tag. He tapped a button on his wrist device. The firm's logo filled the screen. He held it up for Samantha to see.

"I work for Ascenda, too," said Prince.

"We're colleagues?"

"It seems so," said Prince. "How did you get the job?"

"I was lucky, I guess," said Samantha. "In the right place at the right time, as they say. I was walking dogs one afternoon in Charlotte and I met a man who offered me an interview. He hired me. It was some kind of crazy luck."

"Who hired you?"

"Mr. Bromwell," said Samantha. "Do you know him?"

"Yes. Mr. Bromwell hired me, too," said Prince. "He sat down at my table in a crowded coffeehouse and offered me an opportunity. I've never looked back."

"What are the chances that we'd work for the same firm?" said Samantha. "And be hired by the same man? Hmm," she said. "Are you sure you didn't recruit me on the plane?" Samantha smiled.

"I'd like to claim responsibility," said Prince.

"Very diplomatic," said Samantha.

"I've had training."

Samantha smiled.

"Welcome aboard, Samantha," said Prince.

"Thank you, Morgan," said Samantha. "How have you been?"

"Good," said Prince. "I took your advice and contacted my ex-wife about the girls. I've reestablished contact with my younger daughter, Alicia," said Prince.

"Morgan, that's wonderful," said Samantha. "I'm very happy for you. "

"Thanks," said Prince. "My older daughter hasn't yet agreed to meet with me but I'll keep trying."

"She might change her mind."

"I'm hoping," said Prince. "Meeting Alicia has been a blast."

~ 13 ~
New Jersey

Melissa Watson stared at herself in the bathroom mirror.

She touched her swollen eye and winced. She'd have to wear sunglasses again. She pulled up her shirt to examine the purple pattern spreading across her lower back, the result of Jake's savage kicks the night before.

Melissa frowned. She'd have to stay away from the gym until she healed. She sighed. She had just gone back. The membership clerk had been so kind.

"We missed you, Melissa," said the clerk. "Welcome back." Ceci had given Melissa a club towel.

Melissa shook her head. She hurt in so many places.

Melissa stared into the mirror.

"I'm tired of feeling like shit everyday," she said to her reflection.

Melissa Watson signed her daughter out of school. She drove her silver Honda CR-V to the Garden State Mall in Paramus. She led Janie to the food court. She purchased coffee for herself and juice for Janie. They sat at a table in the dining area.

A young man stopped at their table. He nodded at Melissa and placed a bundle of napkins on the table.

Melissa found a set of car keys inside the bundle of napkins. She and Janie followed the young man to a dark green Hyundai Santa Fe parked in a lot outside the mall.

Melissa drove the Hyundai to the Woodrow Wilson Service Center at Exit 7 on the New Jersey Turnpike.

"Honey," she said, to her daughter. "Wake up. Let's get you some lunch."

"I want a hot dog," said Janie, sleepily.

"Then a hot dog it shall be."

Melissa and Janie sat at a table along the windows in the dining area. Janie chomped happily on her hot dog. Melissa stared at the television screen on the wall. Her cell phone buzzed.

She read the text message from her husband.

'Where are you? I called the house. No answer.'

Melissa sucked in her breath. She texted back.

'At the mall with Janie.'

Melissa noticed the weather forecast on the television screen. She typed a new message to Jake.

'Storm this weekend. Shopping for rain boots.'

Her phone buzzed again.

'You don't need new boots.'

Melissa texted her husband back.

'For Janie.'

'Janie doesn't need new boots, either. We'll talk about it tonight.'

Melissa checked the time. She and Janie had been waiting in the Exit 7 Rest Area for over an hour and a half. Her morning connection at the Garden State Mall had been so quick that she had begun to believe that she really could escape her husband. Now, she wasn't sure. She tapped her fingers anxiously on the table.

Janie looked up from her coloring book.

"What's wrong, Mommy?"

"Nothing, honey. I was just thinking."

"Are we going soon?" Janie asked.

"Yes, pretty soon, I think," said Melissa.

"Mommy, can I get ice cream?"

"Yes, you may get ice cream," said Melissa. "A special treat for a special girl on a special trip."

Janie giggled.

Melissa frowned. She glanced nervously around the rest area.

Samantha read the message on her device.

'Exit 7 Plaza. Help abused woman and daughter.'

Samantha entered the Woodrow Wilson Service Center. She followed the line of women into the ladies' room. She searched for her client in the shops on the ends of the rest area. She entered the dining area off the food court.

Samantha spotted a woman and a young girl at a table along the windows. The little girl knelt on her chair, spooning ice cream from a cup. The woman stared down at her phone.

Samantha purchased a cup of coffee and took it to a table across from the two. Samantha smiled at the girl.

"I have ice cream," the girl said. She tilted the cup to show Samantha.

"That looks delicious," said Samantha. "Vanilla is my

favorite flavor."

"Mine, too," said the girl. She ate another spoonful.

"What's your name?" the girl asked.

"My name is Samantha. What's yours?"

"I'm Janie. My mommy is Melissa."

"Janie, finish your ice cream," said Melissa.

"Are you on a special trip?" Janie asked.

Samantha smiled. "You know, I think I am."

Janie smiled. She spooned her ice cream.

The girl's mother locked eyes with Samantha.

"Do you know us?" she asked.

"No," said Samantha. "I don't know you. I'm just having a cup of coffee. I mean no harm."

"Janie, it's time to go."

"But, Mommy," wailed Janie. "I'm not finished with my ice cream."

"We can take it with us. Come on."

Melissa stood from the table. She lifted Janie from her chair. She picked up the ice cream and took Janie's hand. She pulled her through the food court to the exit.

Samantha followed.

Melissa opened the back seat of the Hyundai and lifted Janie into the car seat. She strapped Janie into the seat and kissed her forehead. She closed the car door and turned.

Melissa jumped, surprised to find Samantha standing behind her. Melissa's eyes narrowed.

"Who are you? Why are you following me?" She rounded the front of the vehicle to the driver's door. "Did my husband send you? Did he have me followed?"

"Melissa?" said Samantha. "I don't know your husband. I don't know you, either. But you look nervous and scared. Can I help you?"

Melissa shook her head.

"What's wrong?" said Samantha.

Melissa stared at her. "Someone was supposed to meet me here. I've been waiting a long time. I don't know what to do."

"Where would you go now?"

"Back home, I guess," said Melissa. "If I leave now, I can be home by the time my husband gets home from work. I can pretend that it's just a normal day."

"What happens on a normal day?" asked Samantha.

Melissa sighed. "My husband gets physical," she said. "I left him this morning. The later it gets, the better chance he has of finding me. And, if he finds me, I'm afraid that he'll kill me."

Melissa bit her lip. Tears came to her eyes

"I don't know what to do," she said. "I'm taking my daughter away from her father. Is that the right thing to do?"

"What did you think when you woke up this morning?" asked Samantha.

"I'm tired of being beaten. I'm tired of living in fear. I don't want my daughter to grow up this way."

"Okay," said Samantha. "Let me see if I can help you. Who was supposed to meet you? Can you contact them?"

"No. I'm only supposed to use my phone to communicate with my husband," said Melissa. "The people who are helping me said they'll take my phone somewhere else, and destroy it."

"Your husband can't connect me to you," said Samantha. "I'll contact them on my phone."

Samantha sent Melissa's contact a message.

Her phone quickly buzzed with a response.

'Lila delayed due to traffic below Exit 7. Can you deliver client to the Holiday Inn at Exit 5?'

"Melissa, it's just a traffic delay," said Samantha. She showed Melissa the message. "I'll take you to meet them."

~ 14 ~
Paramus New Jersey

Harry Quigley sat in a green and white vinyl chair outside his apartment in the late afternoon of a warm October day. His dog Jesse, a black Labrador retriever, lay at his feet.

Harry heard the squeak of a screen door. His neighbor, Ceci Torres, stepped onto the landing outside her apartment in the building up the slope from Harry's own.

"Hi, Harry," Ceci called, as she walked along the sidewalk to the parking lot.

"Hi, Ceci," said Harry. "Working tonight?"

"Yes. I'm bartending at Sketch."

"Have a good night," said Harry.

"Thanks. See you, Harry."

Jake Watson arrived home from work to an empty house. Three weeks had passed since his wife and daughter had gone missing. His wife's Honda CR-V had been found in the parking garage of the Garden State Mall. The last ping from his wife's cell phone had come from the town of Benezette, in Elk County, Pennsylvania. The police had no leads.

Jake was impatient to know the truth about his wife's disappearance. He believed that his wife had tried to escape him. He believed that his wife had dared to take his daughter away from him. He seethed.

"What can I get you?" Ceci asked the customer at the bar.

"A gin and tonic," said Jake Watson.

Ceci placed the drink on the bar in front of him.

Jake tossed a ten dollar bill onto the bar.

At three o'clock in the morning. Harry Quigley sat outside his apartment. His dog alerted to the arrival of two cars to the parking lot of the apartment complex.

Ceci Torres pulled her white Honda Civic into her assigned parking space in the lot. A black Range Rover pulled into the empty space next to hers.

Harry heard low chatter between the two cars. He checked the front license plate of the Range Rover, a habit he had developed after spending his career on the police force. The vehicle had a Jersey license plate. Harry could make out the first letter on the plate, H, and the first number, 9.

Ceci got out of her car.

The Range Rover backed out of its parking space and pulled forward. The driver spoke to Ceci through the passenger window. Ceci's laughter carried in the quiet of the early morning. As the driver pulled the vehicle to the corner, Harry caught the last letter on the license plate, R.

Ceci walked unsteadily to her apartment. She fumbled with her keys at the door. She dropped them and teetered as she bent down to pick them up. Ceci grabbed onto the railing to steady herself. She turned the key in the lock and stepped inside the apartment. The porch light popped on.

Jesse barked as a man emerged from the bushes at the end of Ceci's building. The man climbed the two steps to Ceci's landing. He entered the apartment and closed the door. The porch light went out.

The next afternoon, Ceci's roommate, Denise, waved to Harry as she rolled her luggage across the sidewalk.

"Hi Denise. Welcome home."

"Thanks, Harry," said Denise.

"I guess Ceci didn't go to work today," said Harry. "Her car's still here."

Denise glanced at Ceci's car in the lot.

"Well, there's a cold going around," said Denise. "See you, Harry."

Denise entered the apartment.

She came out, screaming.

Harry drove to the hospital to see Ceci that evening. A nurse who had cared for Harry's late wife Edith let him in to visit Ceci in the Intensive Care Unit.

Harry stared down at Ceci's swollen face. A white bandage was wrapped around her head. Bandages covered her broken nose. A cloth had been placed over her eyes to reduce swelling. Her skin was pasty, too pale. She had purple blotches on her neck, arms, and wrists.

Harry took Ceci's hand.

"Hi, Ceci. It's Harry. I just wanted to let you know that I'm here." He squeezed her hand.

"That's right," said a nurse who entered the room. "Talk to her. Sometimes it helps."

"Ceci's my neighbor," said Harry.

"She suffered a terrible assault," said the nurse.

Harry nodded. "I wish I could have prevented it."

Harry sat in the orange vinyl chair against the wall. He listened to the constant ticking of the clock on the wall and the gentle rhythm of Ceci's slow respiration. In the warmth of the hospital room, Harry found himself beginning to doze off.

Harry woke to see a white-coated doctor standing at Ceci's bedside.

"You work late, Doctor," said Harry.

Morgan Prince turned.

"That's the kind of day I've had," said Prince. "I didn't see you there. Are you related to the patient?"

"No. I'm her neighbor. Her parents will be here in the morning," said Harry. "I told them I'd watch her tonight."

"You're a good neighbor."

"I'd like to think we're friends," said Harry. "When my wife Edith passed ten months ago, Ceci was especially kind to me. She didn't deserve this."

"No. She didn't," said Prince. He shook his head. "Well, I suppose I should get to work."

"Oh, certainly, Doctor," said Harry. He sat back down in the chair.

Prince took Ceci's pulse.

He removed the cloth over her eyes and gently touched his fingertips to her closed lids. He gently brushed his fingers down the sides of her bandaged face. He held his hands against the sides of her head.

Prince held his palms above Ceci. He slowly lowered

his hands until his fingers gently touched her bruised torso. He lifted his hands and repeated the motion several times.

"Doctor, are you doing reiki?" Harry whispered.

Prince gripped Ceci's wrists. He uncovered her feet and gripped her ankles.

Prince clasped Ceci's hands in his own. He closed his eyes. Prince again placed his hands on the sides of Ceci's bandaged head.

He stepped back from the hospital bed.

"She needs time to heal," said Prince. "I'd expect that she'll be unconscious for a few days. She'll need time to rest," he said, "but I think she'll make a full recovery."

"Thank you, Doctor," said Harry. "Her parents will be so relieved."

"Good night, sir." Prince left the room.

Harry stopped at the nurse's station on his way out of the hospital.

"Excuse me," he said to the nurse on duty. "I didn't get the name of the doctor who stopped to see Ceci Torres tonight. Can you check it for me? I'd like to let her parents know his name."

The nurse checked the doctor's logs.

"Dr. Jacob was here at six," said the nurse. "He was the last doctor to see Ms. Torres today."

"Are you sure?" said Harry. "He was here about twenty minutes ago."

The nurse glanced back at her computer screen.

"I'm sorry," she said. "No other doctor signed in tonight."

"Hmm. Okay," said Harry. "Well, thank you for checking. I'm headed home. Have a good evening."

Harry Quigley listened to the news broadcast on the radio. His dog Jesse slept at his feet.

"Police have arrested a suspect in the savage assault that took place in a Paramus apartment complex," said the news reporter. "Police credit an observant witness who captured partial license plate information for a vehicle that arrived home with the victim on the night of her assault," said the reporter.

"Police were able to match the plate to a black Range Rover owned by Mr. Jake Watson, an area vice president for Intech Mobile. Witnesses have placed Mr. Watson at a local bar with the victim. Evidence obtained at the crime scene links Mr. Watson to the assault.

"Mr. Watson recently reported the disappearance of his wife and child," said the reporter. "With tonight's arrest, police tell us that they are concerned that Mr. Watson may have harmed his family."

Melissa Watson watched television as she folded laundry in the common room of the women's shelter in Baltimore. When she returned to her room in the shelter, she found a note slipped under the door. She unfolded the slip of paper.

Jake Watson arrested for assault on woman in Paramus. Victim in critical condition in Hackensack Hospital."

~ 15 ~

Paramus, New Jersey

Harry Quigley sat outside in the afternoon sunshine, listening to the baseball game on the radio. Jesse lay at his feet.

A white Bentley pulled into an empty spot in the parking lot of the apartment complex. The driver got out of the vehicle. He was dressed in a black suit and a peach tie. He adjusted his tie in the side mirror of the car.

Harry checked the Bentley. There was no plate on the front of the vehicle.

The man whistled as he walked along the sidewalk toward Harry.

Jesse barked as the man approached.

The man stopped on the sidewalk. He held up his hands. "I mean no harm."

Harry petted the dog's head. "Jesse, sit."

The dog sank to the ground.

"Are you Harry Quigley?" asked the man.

"Who wants to know?" said Harry.

"I'm David Bromwell." He pulled a business card from the pocket of his suit jacket and handed it to Harry.

Harry fingered the two red italic letters on the glossy

black background of the business card.

"What's this about?" said Harry.

"I understand that you provided partial plate information that led to the arrest of a suspect in an assault that took place here." Mr. Bromwell's gaze tracked to the end unit of the apartment building opposite Harry's own.

"I'm a retired detective," said Harry. "I've developed a habit of checking plates. The police did the hard work. They matched the plate and identified the suspect."

"You're a modest man, Mr. Quigley," said Mr. Bromwell.

"I wish I could have prevented the assault."

"You couldn't have known," said Mr. Bromwell. "I understand that you were injured in the line of duty when you were on the police force."

"Yes. I was injured in a jewelry store heist," said Harry. "A bullet nicked my lung. The doctors told me I was lucky to survive."

"Is that when you retired?"

"No," said Harry. "Once I recuperated, I went back to work. I retired when my wife Edith got sick. She passed ten months ago."

"I'm sorry for your loss," said Mr. Bromwell.

"Thank you," said Harry. "Now, what's this about?"

"Mr. Quigley, I run a state of the art security operation," said Mr. Bromwell. "We provide a combination of technology and talent that's unmatched in our industry. I could use your observational skills for advance work on certain projects," he said.

"Would you be open to considering part-time employment with my firm?"

"Jesse," said Harry. "I believe this man is offering me a job."

~ 16 ~

Washington Square Park, New York City

Morgan Prince relaxed on a bench in Washington Square Park. He admired the inventive Halloween costumes worn by people on their way to the Greenwich Village parade.

Prince had arrived in the city after completing a job in Jersey City, hopeful that he could meet with his daughter Alicia. His ex-wife told him that Alicia had hockey practice and then had plans to go to a Halloween party at a friend's home.

Prince stared up at the branches of a towering oak tree in the middle of the sparse park lawn.

A jogger stopped and followed his gaze.

"What are you looking at?" she asked.

"I'm just appreciating that tree," said Prince, chuckling.

"Oh. I thought that maybe you'd spotted a rare bird."

"No." Prince smiled. "Hi. I'm Morgan Prince."

"Hi. I'm Ellen. Do you live here?"

"No. I'm just visiting. My daughters live here," said Prince. "Do you?"

"Yes. I live just a few blocks south of here," said Ellen.

A costumed skeleton trio passed by.

"Happy Halloween," said Prince. "I've seen some great

costumes tonight. Do you have plans to celebrate?"

"No. My only plans this evening are to finish my run, to order Chinese food, and to stay in. Halloween isn't one of my favorite days. It's my birthday," she said.

"I guess Halloween would be a tough day for a birthday. Same as Christmas, I think," said Prince. "Happy Birthday."

"It's not so happy," said Ellen. "I turned thirty today. My life is over."

"Not true," said Prince. "You have so much more to explore in your life."

"I haven't enjoyed my recent experiences," said Ellen, shaking her head. "Who says that I'll enjoy the future?"

"What were your recent experiences?" Prince asked.

"Last week, my boyfriend moved out. It was hard enough making rent when I was splitting it with my boyfriend. I lost my job three hours ago. I don't know what I'm going to do now. And, to top it all off, I'm thirty."

"Ellen, I'm sorry that things haven't gone as you had hoped," said Prince. "But you can always get a new job. And you can always find a new boyfriend. And, trust me, your life isn't over at thirty," he said. "Just pursue what makes you happy. Focus on the positive. Everything else will fall into place."

"Hmm. Maybe."

"Can I buy you a drink to celebrate your birthday?"

"Oh, thank you. No," said Ellen, shaking her head. "That's kind of you, but I've got to finish my run."

"Just one drink," said Prince. "I'd like to wish you well in the future. Nothing more than that."

"You're very kind. I just don't think that I'm in the right frame of mind for it," said Ellen. "I'm just going to finish my run and go home. It was nice to meet you, Mr. Prince. Enjoy your visit."

"Happy Birthday, Ellen."

Steve Owens entered the pass code on the security panel outside Ellen's apartment building. He climbed the stairs to the fifth floor and knocked lightly on Ellen's door. Until last week, it had been his door, too.

Steve waited at the door. He knocked again. He called Ellen's cell phone. The call went to voice mail. He left a message.

"Hi, Ellen, it's Steve. I'm at your door. I wanted to wish you a Happy Birthday. Let me in." He ended the call.

Steve found the apartment key on his key ring and slid it into the lock. He pushed the door open and entered the apartment.

"Ellen?" Steve called. He walked through the dark living room. He glanced inside the empty kitchen. He walked down the hallway.

Steve turned the knob on Ellen's bedroom door. He pushed the door open. The bedroom was empty.

Steve turned the knob on the bathroom door. He pushed the door open. Candles flickered in the room. The shower curtain was closed over the bath.

"Ellen? It's me, Steve. Are you in here?"

"Ellen?" said Steve.

He stared at the curtain over the bathtub.

"Ellen?"

Steve pushed the curtain aside.

Ellen lay in the bathtub, her eyes closed, her head resting against the end of the tub. Blood seeped from her wrists into the tub of pink water.

Steve touched his fingers to Ellen's neck. He felt a pulse. He dialed 911.

~ 17 ~
Freeport, New York

Jamal stocked yogurt in the dairy aisle of the Stop and Shop Supermarket. Vanessa approached him in the aisle.

"Congratulations on being picked for the art trip," said Vanessa. "Where is it?"

"Dallas," said Jamal.

"Wow. Your Gran must be proud," said Vanessa.

"She is," said Jamal, "but she's worried, too."

"Why? You went to Florida."

"Yes, and she worried," said Jamal. "That's just Gran."

"When is the trip" Vanessa asked.

"It's not until spring," said Jamal.

"I guess that will give your Gran sometime to get used to the idea," said Vanessa.

"It also gives me time to save up for it. I'm going to ask Mr. Zachary for more hours."

"Good luck," said Vanessa. "Okay. I'll see you later, Jamal. I'm on my break."

~ 18 ~
Freeport, New York

The lines at each of the open registers in the Freeport Stop and Shop snaked into the aisles as customers gathered last-minute supplies for their New Year's Eve celebrations. The night manager yelled out from the customer service desk.

"Jamal, close down!"

"Yes, Mr. Zachary," said Jamal. He turned off the register light on Lane #8.

Jamal's coworker Vanessa placed a Closed sign on Jamal's conveyor belt and steered Jamal's last two customers to her line. Jamal scanned the purchases of his remaining customers.

"Happy New Year," Jamal said to his last customer. He opened his register to clock out for the night.

A woman placed a loaf of bread on his conveyor belt.

"I'm closed, Ma'am," said Jamal. "You can take that to the express lines at the end." Jamal pointed to the registers near the store exit.

The woman picked up the loaf of bread and placed it down near the scanner on Jamal's belt. She read his name tag.

"Jamal, I just have one loaf of bread," she said. "Can't you take me?"

"Ma'am, my shift has ended," said Jamal. "I need to clock out. I'm sorry. The express lines move quickly."

Samantha glanced up at the clerk. "Jamal?"

Jamal squinted at her. He nodded in recognition.

"Samantha? From the plane?" he said.

Samantha nodded. "Yes. I can't believe it's you," she said.

"I live here, Samantha," said Jamal. "Why are you here?"

"I'm on assignment for a new job," said Samantha.

"In Freeport? What kind of job?" Jamal asked.

"I work for a security firm," said Samantha.

"Are you on stake out? Are you making sandwiches?"

Samantha chuckled. "No. I've been assigned a training task tonight," she said. "I had no idea that I'd run into you."

Mr. Zachary appeared at the end of Jamal's lane.

"Jamal, are you clocking out, or what? Let's go!"

"Just this last customer, Mr. Zachary."

Jamal scanned Samantha's loaf of bread.

"That's three dollars," he said.

Mr. Zachary walked back to the customer service booth

Samantha handed Jamal a single dollar bill.

Jamal read the message that was scrawled across the bill in purple marker pen.

'Don't get into a car tonight.'

Samantha handed him a second dollar bill.

He read the message written in green marker pen.

'Stay home tonight.'

Samantha handed him the last dollar bill.

Jamal read the message scrawled in blue marker pen.

'Live to see the New Year.'

Jamal shuffled through the bills. He shook his head.

"Samantha, did you write on these?" he asked.

"I did," said Samantha. "I want you to stay home tonight, Jamal. New Year's Eve is a bad night to be on the roads."

"I've already made plans," said Jamal, shaking his head.

"Jamal, I'd seriously ask you to cancel those plans," said Samantha. "Live to see the New Year, Jamal." Samantha picked up the loaf of bread. She turned to go.

"Wait," said Jamal.

Samantha turned back. "What is it, Jamal?"

"On the plane, I heard you talking with the man in the aisle seat," he said.

"Morgan Prince."

"Yes, okay. I heard you talking about waking up from your coma," said Jamal. "And I heard Mr. Prince say that his doctors called his death."

"Yes?" said Samantha.

"I think I'm like both of you," said Jamal.

"Like us? What do you mean?"

"On the plane, you asked me if I could make it 'three for three'. I think that I can," said Jamal.

Samantha squinted at him. "How?"

"I survived my mother's fall down brick and concrete steps when she was pregnant with me," said Jamal. "And I think that I drowned when I was five but, somehow, I was found alive on the river bank. I have no idea how I got there. I think I'm like you."

"It was 'three for three', after all?" said Samantha.

Jamal nodded. "I think so."

"Imagine that," said Samantha. "What are the odds?"

Jamal shrugged.

"Well, Jamal, if that's the case," said Samantha, "then maybe you should pay extra attention to the messages on those bills. Be safe tonight, Jamal."

"Jamal, let's go!" yelled Mr. Zachary.

"I'm coming, Mr. Zachary."

Jamal swapped out the three defaced dollar bills with

three single bills from his own wallet. He removed his till to clock out for the night.

A wave of lightheadedness hit Jamal as he waited for his friends in the parking lot of the Seven-Eleven on Merrick Road. Jamal lowered his head between his knees and rocked back and forth.

Jack and Denny pulled up in Jack's black Mustang Convertible. Jack lowered the driver's window.

"Jamal, what's up with you?" Jack asked.

"Are you already lit?" asked Denny. He sat in the passenger seat of Jack's car.

"I think I'm sick."

"Aw, man," said Jack. "Really?"

"I don't feel well," said Jamal. "I think I'm just going to go home. I'm sorry, Jack."

"All right, I get it," said Jack. "Can I give you a lift home?"

"No. Thanks. I'll walk. It's just down the street," said Jamal. "Have fun tonight. Happy New Year."

"Happy New Year," said Jack.

"Later," said Denny.

Vanessa's phone call woke Jamal early on New Year's Day.

Jamal found his grandmother in the kitchen.

"Happy New Year, Jamal," said Nora.

"Happy New Year, Gran."

"Are you feeling any better this morning?" Nora asked. "I'm making pancakes for breakfast."

"Gran, Vanessa just called," said Jamal. "She told me that Jack and Denny died in a car accident on their way home last night. A Ford 150 drove into the back of Jack's Mustang at the drawbridge on the Loop Parkway."

"Oh, my," said Nora, clutching her bathrobe. "Jamal, I'm very sorry for the loss of your friends," she said. "That's terrible news to start the new year."

"Gran, I keep thinking that, if I hadn't been sick last night, I would have been with them," said Jamal. "And I would have been sitting in the back seat."

"Jamal, don't talk like that," said Nora. "It's a blessing that you weren't in that car last night."

"Gran, I think that I was warned to stay home."

"Warned? Who warned you, Jamal?" Nora asked.

Jamal pulled the three dollar bills from the pocket of his bathrobe. He gave them to his grandmother.

"A customer paid with these bills last night," said Jamal.

Nora read through the messages on the bills.

"Jamal, what is this?"

"Gran, the customer who paid with these bills last night is the same lady from the flight to Florida. The lady who woke from the coma," he said.

"Last night, she came into the store. She said that she was on a training assignment for a new job with a security firm," said Jamal. "Her instructions were to persuade the clerk on Lane #8 to stay home last night. She said that she didn't know it would be me."

Nora reread the messages on the dollar bills.

"Is that why you weren't feeling well last night?"

"I think it got to me," said Jamal. "I was warned to stay home and I did. I lived. Gran, why was I saved?"

"Jamal, it's a blessing that you were saved," said Nora. "Just accept the blessing."

~ 19 ~

Greenwich Village, New York City

Morgan and Alicia Prince walked the streets of Greenwich Village on a brisk Saturday afternoon.

"Did you know that Gwen's graduating from high school this year?" said Alicia.

"Yes," said Morgan. "Time passes by so quickly."

"Gwen got into four colleges," said Alicia. "Do you know where she wants to go?"

"I don't," said Morgan.

"NYU," said Alicia. "Can you believe that?"

"It's an excellent school," said Morgan. "Gaining acceptance to NYU is quite an accomplishment. Your sister must have worked very hard."

"I guess," said Alicia.

"Are you a good student?"

"I'm average," said Alicia. "But I have a lot of extracurricular activity."

Alicia stopped in front of the Brewster Tea Shop.

"My mom gets tea here," she said. Bells jingled as Alicia opened the door of the shop. "Hi, Neil," she called.

"Hello, Alicia. Do you need anything today?"

"Thanks. Not today," said Alicia. "We're just out for a walk. Neil, this is my birth father Morgan. Morgan, Neil is the manager of the shop."

Alicia waved. "Bye, Neil." She pulled the door closed.

Morgan and Alicia crossed the street.

"Gwen's going to live on the NYU campus," said Alicia. "Don't you think that's weird, since we live so close?"

Morgan smiled. "Living on campus is part of the college experience," he said. "It sounds to me like maybe you're going to miss your sister."

"She's a pain," said Alicia, "but I'm used to having her around. It won't be the same."

"Well, you'll have to find other ways to keep in touch."

"You don't know Gwen," said Alicia, shaking her head. "College is her chance to get away from me."

"That can't be true," said Morgan. "College is only four years. Sisters are forever. I'm sure that Gwen's just excited to graduate from high school and go on to college."

"She pretends that she's not excited," said Alicia, "but I know that she is."

"She should be excited," said Morgan. "She has a great future ahead of her. You will, too, when you graduate, Alicia."

"I'm going away to school," said Alicia.

"Well, everyone is different," said Morgan. "You and Gwen are sisters but you have very different personalities. As it should be," he said. "Where would you go?"

"I don't know," said Alicia. "Alaska, maybe."

"Interesting choice," said Morgan.

"Or California," said Alicia. "Or Nebraska."

"Well, I guess that you have some time to consider it."

Morgan and Alicia walked through the Arch into Washington Square Park.

"My Mom said we might go to Paris when Gwen graduates," said Alicia.

"That would be a fantastic graduation present," said Morgan. "Paris is a wonderful destination."

"Have you been there?"

"I have, but only for work," said Prince. "It was a quick trip. I saw the Eiffel Tower in the distance."

"I hope we go," said Alicia.

~ 20 ~
Dallas, Texas

Samantha stood on the lawn of the outdoor garden at the Nasher Sculpture Center in Dallas. She reread her message.

'Bomber in gray hoodie.'

Samantha glanced at the visitors in the garden.

An older couple admired a Henry Moore Sculpture at the back of the garden. A mother took a picture of her young boys standing between rush hour commuters. A student group was identifiable by their matching lanyard tags.

Samantha noticed the man standing in the back of a line of people who were waiting to enter an installation akin to a steel tepee. Visitors entered the narrow space and walked along a graveled path through its center to exit onto the grass on the opposite side.

The man at the back of the line wore a gray hoodie. He stared down at his phone, swiping at its screen. He fidgeted.

Samantha tapped a student on the shoulder. She read his name tag when he turned.

"Jamal," she said. She stared at him.

"Samantha?"

"Jamal?"

"You know her?" said Jamal's friend.

"Yes. Hi, Samantha," said Jamal. "This is my friend Louis. Louis, this is Samantha."

"Jamal, can you help me?"

"What do you need?"

"See that guy over there in the gray hoodie?" said Samantha. "I think he's got a bomb on him. I'm going into that installation after him. Would you alert museum security?"

Jamal glanced at the man in the gray hoodie. "Okay."

"And, would you have your friends start ushering people out of the garden without alarming them?"

"What should they say?" said Louis.

"Tell them that the museum needs to do maintenance on the lawn for fifteen minutes," said Samantha. "Go!"

Samantha pushed ahead of the people in the line to enter the steel tepee. Inside, she pushed ahead of the people in front of her. She moved ahead of a man and his two young girls.

She saw the man in the gray hoodie in the center of the piece. He knelt down on the gravel to tie his sneakers. He tossed something down onto the rocks. He stood and glanced around.

Samantha lunged at him, knocking him down onto the gravel. He scrambled up and away from her. He kicked at her head. He reached the exit.

Samantha emerged from the installation to find that Jamal and Louis had tackled the man as he exited. The man's cell phone had flown up and fallen in the grass.

Museum security surrounded them.

"Get them off me," said the man in the hoodie.

"No! Hold him!" said Samantha. "He planted a bomb inside." She found the man's phone in the grass. She tapped on its screen.

"That's private property!" the man yelled.

"Here it is," said Samantha. "Good. We got lucky," she said. "It's not on a timer."

Samantha gave the man's phone to the Dallas police. She described the location of the bomb for the bomb squad.

"Jamal and Louis, thank you for helping me today," said Samantha. "Thank you for alerting security and for having your friends usher people out of the garden. I have to say that I wasn't expecting you to tackle the guy."

"We just wanted to make sure he didn't get away," said Louis. "Jamal and I are on the football team. We're used to tackling guys."

Samantha smiled. "If I didn't get him, I expected the police to catch him," she said. "Not the two of you. But, thank you."

Louis spied a Channel Eight reporter walking down the steps of the Nasher Museum Café.

"Jamal," said Louis, "I'm going to get us on TV."

"Jamal, what are you doing here?" asked Samantha.

"We're on a school art trip," said Jamal.

"So, you are an artist, after all," said Samantha.

"I applied to college, Samantha," said Jamal. "I'm going to NYU in the fall."

"That's great, Jamal. Congratulations. College can open a whole new world for you."

Jamal nodded. He squinted at Samantha.

"Samantha, how did you know that my friends would be in an accident on New Year's Eve?"

"I didn't know, Jamal," she said. "I was working. I was following my instructions. I'm very sorry about your friends."

"I stayed home and lived," said Jamal.

"I'm glad that I was able to persuade you."

Jamal frowned.

"Did you know that it was me today when you tapped me on the shoulder?" he asked.

"No," said Samantha. "I needed to stop the guy and I needed someone to alert museum security. I couldn't do both."

"So, it was just a coincidence?"

"It seems so," said Samantha. "I'm very surprised to run into you here."

"When I met you on the plane, I never thought that I would see you again," said Jamal. "Since then, I've run into you twice. The first time, you saved my life. Was that just coincidence?"

"I don't know, Jamal," said Samantha.

"Are we connected because we survived nearly fatal incidents?" said Jamal. "Do you think that's why we met?"

Samantha shrugged. "I don't know, Jamal."

"I don't understand it," said Jamal.

"Jamal, don't worry about it," said Samantha. "You're going to college. Just work hard and do good things."

Jamal squinted at her.

"My father said that."

"It's good advice, Jamal."

Samantha glanced over Jamal's shoulder.

"I've got to get out of here before Louis brings that television crew over to us," Samantha said. "Thank you for helping me today, Jamal. Perhaps we'll meet again soon."

Jamal called his grandmother that night.

"Jamal, we saw you on the news!" said Nora.

"In New York?"

"Yes. They showed you and Louis in your football uniforms. I'm proud of you."

"Gran, we just tackled the guy. He would have been

caught, anyway."

"Jamal, you did a good thing," said Nora. "You helped to save lives today."

"I guess," said Jamal.

"What's wrong?" said Nora.

"Louis and I tackled that guy to help Samantha. The lady from the flight to Florida. The lady who told me to stay home on New Year's," said Jamal. "Today, she was at the museum in Dallas. She tapped me on the shoulder and asked me to let museum security know that she needed help."

"And you helped her," said Nora. "Jamal, you did a good thing today."

"I know," said Jamal. "I just don't understand why I keep running into Samantha. Is it just coincidence?"

"I don't know, Jamal," said Nora.

"What if it's not?" said Jamal.

~ 21 ~
New Orleans, Louisiana

Morgan Prince stood at the end of the platform for the New Orleans Riverfront Line. Two men sat together on the railing at the opposite end. A young man arrived. He stared down at his phone as he waited in the middle of the platform. The two men got up from the railing.

Prince reached the young man before the men did. One of the men pulled out a knife. "Your wallets," he said.

Prince kicked out at the man. He delivered a blow to the man's hand holding the knife. It clattered to the platform. Prince delivered a blow to the man's neck. The man crumpled. His partner took off running.

"Are you okay?" Prince asked the young man.

"Yes. Thank you. How did you do that?"

"I've had training. Hi. I'm Morgan Prince."

"I'm Steve Owens."

"Call 911," said Prince. "Let the police take care of this guy. Maybe they'll find his friend."

Steve reported the incident.

"A car's on its way," he told Prince. He stared at the man lying on the platform. "Do you think he would have cut us?"

"I don't know," said Prince. "He won't, now."

"Thank you, Mr. Prince."

"I'm glad that I could help," said Prince.

Steve Owens delivered a draft Abita to Prince at the Charles Street Tavern.

"Thank you for helping me tonight, Mr. Prince."

"It was my pleasure," said Prince. "How long have you been in New Orleans, Steve? You don't sound like you're from here."

"I just moved here at the beginning of the year," said Steve. "Before that, I lived in New York City."

"My daughters live in the city. Why did you move here?"

"I had a bad experience in the city," said Steve. "I came here to forget about it for a while."

Steve served two customers at the bar. He returned to Prince.

"Can I ask what happened in the city?"

"Hmm," said Steve. He shook his head.

"I found my ex-girlfriend after she attempted to kill herself. I can't stop thinking about it," said Steve. "That's why I'm here."

"I'm sorry," said Prince. "That sounds like a traumatic experience. How are you doing?"

"I don't know if you ever get over something like that," said Steve, "but I'm trying. The distance helps."

"How's your ex-girlfriend?"

"The doctors said that she was lucky that I came along when I did. She's in therapy now."

"You saved her."

"I'm no hero," said Steve. "I broke up with her the week before her birthday. She turned thirty on Halloween. I knew that she'd be upset. When she didn't answer any of my texts that day, I went to her apartment to check on her."

"She turned thirty on Halloween?" said Prince. "And you two broke up the week before? What's her name?"

"Ellen."

"Does Ellen jog in Washington Square Park?"

"Yes. We used to jog there together when we were a couple," said Steve. "Why?"

"I met her in the park on Halloween night," said Prince.

"You met her that night?" said Steve, squinting at Prince.

"Yes. She told me that Halloween was her birthday and she had turned thirty. She told me that she and her boyfriend had broken up the week before. She was sad. She told me that she couldn't envision a happy future for herself."

Prince frowned. "She tried to kill herself that night?"

Steve nodded.

"I knew that she was sad but I failed to understand the extent of her depression," said Prince. "I failed her." He sighed. "But she's okay?"

"Yes. She pulled through. She's getting help."

"You saved her, Steve," said Prince.

Samantha sat a table in the Bourbon Street Café in the French Quarter. A jazz band played in the center of the brightly lit room. A small dance floor in front of the band divided the sparse crowd.

A couple sat at a table three rows ahead of Samantha, the only other table occupied on the left side of the bar. The woman at the table was older than her male companion by at least twenty years. The woman wore a sparkling red dress and red high heels. A platinum wig was slightly askew on her head.

The woman got up from her seat and danced alone on

the small dance floor. She drunkenly called out to the band members, complimenting them on their performance.

She twirled on the floor.

She lost her balance.

The woman stumbled forward.

Her companion caught her, before she crashed into the band's audio equipment. He guided the woman back to their table.

The band took a break.

Without the music playing, conversations echoed in the room. Samantha overheard the conversation between the man and woman at the table ahead of her.

"Let's go," said the man.

"Let's have one more drink here," said the woman.

The man bought her another drink. "Drink up," he said, "then we're going."

The woman gulped it down. She dropped the glass as she attempted to place it back on the table.

The glass shattered on the floor.

"That's it. Let's go," said the man.

He helped the woman onto her feet. He put his arm around her shoulders, holding her up, as he guided her down the aisle to the exit.

The man's eyes narrowed as he caught Samantha's eyes on him as they approached her table. He pulled the woman closer to him.

Samantha glanced away.

The man opened the door with his shoulder and helped the woman step through the doorway. He held the door open until Samantha glanced up at him. He winked, then let the door close behind him.

The couple walked arm in arm up Bourbon Street.

Samantha sipped coffee in the Café du Monde on Jackson Square in New Orleans.

The host led a customer to a nearby table. The man took a seat at the table, facing Samantha.

Samantha squinted at him, recognizing him.

"Morgan?"

He squinted back at her.

"Samantha?"

"Hi. What a nice surprise. Would you like to join me?" Samantha asked.

"Yes. I'd love to," said Morgan. He slid into a seat at Samantha's table. "What a wonderful surprise to see you, too."

The server arrived to take Prince's order.

"I've thought of you so many times since seeing you in Las Vegas," said Prince. "I'm still amazed that we work for the same company."

"I am, too," said Samantha. "We talked about your job on the plane and then I got approached for a job in the security industry. It's unbelievable that we're colleagues." She smiled. "Maybe you recruited me on the plane."

"I'd like to take credit for it."

"Very diplomatic," said Samantha.

"I've been trained," said Morgan, smiling. "How is the job going?"

"So far, I like it," said Samantha.

"Are you working now?" asked Morgan.

"No. I finished a job in Dallas yesterday. I just came for a visit until I'm reassigned. How about you? Are you working?"

"I finished a job here last night," said Morgan. "Like you, I'm waiting to be reassigned."

"Well, I hope that we can enjoy our breakfast before either one of us is called away," said Samantha.

The wait clerk brought Morgan's order.

Morgan bit into a beignet. "That's good," he said.

"Morgan, do you remember Jamal from the plane?" Samantha asked.

"The guy in the window seat?" said Morgan.

"Yes. Have you run into him since the flight?"

"No," said Morgan, "although, I'm not sure that I'd recognize him if I did. Why?"

"I've run into him twice since the flight," said Samantha. "Jamal was my client on New Year's Eve. And I just ran into him on a job in Dallas. He helped me there." Samantha shook her head. "It's weird."

"Jamal was your client?" said Prince.

"Yes. I was assigned to persuade a clerk to stay home on New Year's Eve. The clerk happened to be Jamal," said Samantha. "When I saw him in Dallas, he told me that he stayed home that night. His friends died in a car crash."

"You successfully persuaded him."

"Yes," said Samantha. "But I find myself wondering what would have happened if I hadn't been successful. Would Jamal have died that night, or would the company have assigned somebody else to intervene?"

"I suppose the firm might have a contingency plan."

"When I saw Jamal on New Year's Eve," said Samantha, "He told me that he thinks he's like us."

"Like us?" asked Prince.

"Jamal heard us talking on the plane," said Samantha. "He thinks that he drowned in a canoe accident but, somehow, survived. He told me that I was right. All three of us survived nearly fatal incidents. What are the chances?"

Morgan frowned. "All three of us?"

"Apparently, so," said Samantha. "I tapped Jamal on the shoulder in Dallas to ask for his help. I had no idea that he was there."

"Why was he there?"

"He was on a school trip," said Samantha. "I asked him to alert the museum guards to an issue at an installation. When I chased the bomber out of the installation, I found that Jamal and his friend had tackled him. Jamal's friend said that they didn't want the guy to get away," she said.

"Jamal said that he doesn't understand why we've run into each other in odd circumstances since the flight. He asked me if we were connected because we both survived death."

Samantha and Morgan sipped their coffee.

"Samantha, I had a bit of a strange encounter myself last night," said Morgan. "I was assigned to a mugging. That's odd in itself, because it's been years since I've been assigned to a mugging. After the police arrived on the scene, I accompanied my client to his job tending bar," he said.

"We discovered that we had a connection in common in New York City," said Prince. "His ex-girlfriend Ellen. I met her in the park on her birthday. My client told me that she tried to kill herself later that night. My client saved her," said Prince.

"If I hadn't been assigned to him that night, I'd never have known what happened that night. It's made me wonder if maybe the firm is sending me a message."

"A message?" said Samantha.

"Maybe the firm set me up with an easy mugging to let me know that I had failed Ellen that night."

"Was she your client?" said Samantha.

"No," said Morgan. "But I should have done more to help her that night."

"What would you have done differently?"

"For starters, I wouldn't have let her out of my sight," said Prince. "I would have stuck with her." He shook his head. "But I let her go."

Samantha frowned. "I feel like I should have done more

to help someone last night," she said. "She wasn't my client, either, but I feel like I should have done more."

"What happened?" said Morgan.

"This younger guy was with an older woman in a bar. The woman was clearly drunk. I got a bad feeling about him. They left together. I feel like I should have done more to help her."

"What would you have done differently?"

"I would have followed them up the street and somehow persuaded the woman to come with me," said Samantha. "I would have gotten her away from that man. Instead, I let her go." She frowned.

"But you don't know that anything bad happened to her," said Morgan. "She may just be nursing a bad hangover today."

"I can only hope that's the case," said Samantha.

~ 22 ~
New Orleans, Louisiana

Steve Owens stocked the ice chest at the Charles Street Tavern in preparation for the Friday evening Happy Hour.

A customer entered the bar, sharply dressed in a navy suit and a lilac tie. He took a seat at the end of the bar.

Steve placed a coaster in front of him.

"Hello, sir. What can I get you?"

"May I have a club soda with lime, please?"

Steve prepared the drink and placed it on the bar.

The man paid with a twenty dollar bill.

Steve read the message that had been scrawled across the note.

'Is this your future?'

Steve made change and continued with his preparations. He stowed a case of beer on the counter underneath the bar. He checked the audio system. He leaned back against the ice chest and nodded, his preparations complete.

"Can I get you anything else?" Steve asked the customer.

"Can we have a conversation?"

"What's on your mind, sir?" said Steve.

"First, please let me introduce myself. I'm David Bromwell." He handed Steve his business card.

"I'm Steve Owens." Steve glanced at the card. "What does 'AS' stand for?"

"Ascenda Security," said Mr. Bromwell. "I manage a security firm."

"Oh. Okay." Steve placed the card on the bar. "What did you want to talk about, Mr. Bromwell?"

"Can I ask how you got started as a bartender, Steve?"

"My dad took bartending lessons so that he could get a second job at night," said Steve. "I helped him study. We learned the drinks and made them together. It was fun."

"Did your father get a job tending bar?"

"Yes. He worked a few nights a week. I went with him sometimes on Saturdays if he had an early shift. I learned a lot from watching him work. My first job was tending bar. I've been doing it ever since."

"Is tending bar your future?"

Steve squinted at him, frowning.

"How long do you see yourself tending bar?"

"I don't know. I haven't given it much thought."

"Let me ask you this. If you envisioned another path for yourself right at this moment," said Mr. Bromwell, "what would it be?"

"There are so many possibilities." Steve shrugged. "I guess maybe I'd go back to New York City and go to college, if I could. Why do you ask?"

"I'm always on the lookout for talent for my firm," said Mr. Bromwell. "What if I offered you an opportunity to work for my firm in New York City and to go to college? Would you take it?"

Steve chuckled. "Sure," he said. He snapped his fingers. "Abracadabra."

"Mr. Owens, please consider it a serious proposal," said

Mr. Bromwell. "Think of it as a work/study program. You would attend college and work part-time for my firm, running odd jobs when needed, and when your schedule permits."

"Work/study?" Steve picked up the business card from the bar.

"The offer comes with assistance in gaining acceptance to college and in financing your education," said Mr. Bromwell. "How does that sound?"

"Honestly, it sounds too good to be true," said Steve. "Why me?"

"Mr. Owens, my business is about saving lives. You've demonstrated that capacity."

"How?" said Steve.

"I understand that you tried to save your parents' lives in a fire," said Mr. Bromwell. "And you recently saved the life of a potential suicide."

"How do you know that?"

"Mr. Owens, my firm is a top-notch security outfit. We do extensive research on potential talent."

Steve shook his head.

"I wasn't able to save my parents," he said. "By the time I got inside the house, it was too late. I fell unconscious from smoke inhalation. I survived but my parents didn't."

"I'm very sorry for your loss."

"Thank you," said Steve. "It was a long time ago but I still feel guilty about it. I keep wondering whether things would have turned out differently if I had stayed home that night."

"Unfortunately, we can't change the past," said Mr. Bromwell. "We can only change our futures."

Steve nodded.

"When I learned that you had saved the life of your ex-girlfriend, I wanted to meet you."

"I'm just glad that I was able to help her."

"You have a promising track record, Mr. Owens," said Mr. Bromwell. "I think you would be well-suited to a position with my firm. I'd like to invest in your future."

Mr. Bromwell stood up from the bar.

"If you're interested in exploring the opportunity further, please call the number on the back of my card. My assistant Krista will take care of the details," he said. "Thank you for the conversation."

~ 23 ~
Greenwich Village, New York City

Bells jingled as Morgan and Alicia entered the Brewster Tea Shop. The clerk behind the counter of the shop closed the book she had been reading and stood to greet them.

"Hello. Can I help you with anything?"

"My Mom gave me a list," said Alicia.

"Okay. Let's see." The clerk lifted the hinged board at the counter and stepped through it.

"Green is over here," she said. She led them to the first aisle marked off by barrels of loose tea. The clerk scooped tea leaves into a bag.

"Oolong is over here." The clerk scooped an oolong tea selection from a barrel. She closed the lid on the barrel

"Okay, one more," she said. "That will be over here." She led them to the second aisle.

Prince stared at the clerk. "You look familiar," he said. "Have we met?"

The clerk squinted at him. She shrugged. "I don't think so," she said. "Are you a regular customer?"

"No," said Prince. "This is my first time."

The clerk shrugged. She took the tea selections to the

counter. She lifted the hinged board and stepped behind the cash register. She rang up the tea purchases.

"Wait. We have met," said Prince. "I remember you now. I met you in Washington Square Park on Halloween. Ellen, right? Do you remember me?"

Ellen squinted at him.

"Oh. Yes I remember now." She nodded. "You're the man who was looking up at the tree."

"Yes. That's me," said Prince. "Morgan Prince."

"You know each other?" said Alicia.

"Ellen, this is my daughter Alicia. Alicia, this is Ellen."

"Hi," said Ellen.

"What an amazing coincidence to run into you again," said Prince. "I recently ran into Steve Owens in New Orleans. He told me what happened that night."

"How do you know Steve?" Ellen asked.

"I met him in New Orleans about a month ago," said Prince. "He told me why he left New York. I realized that he was talking about you." Prince shook his head.

"He left because of me," said Ellen. "How is he doing?"

"He says he's adjusting to New Orleans," said Prince, "but he still misses New York."

Ellen nodded, frowning. "I owe him my life," she said.

"I knew that you were sad that night but I failed to understand the extent of your depression. I never should have let you go that night."

"It's not your fault, Mr. Prince," said Ellen. "You tried to cheer me up. You offered to buy me a drink to celebrate my birthday," she said. She shook her head. "By the time I met you, I was just too far down the road to turn back," she said.

"Anyway, things are much better now. I'm working again, as you can see."

"Good," said Prince. "I hope things continue to improve

for you. Be well, Ellen."

Prince followed Alicia to the door. The bells hanging from the doorknob jingled as they left the shop.

Alicia squinted at Prince outside the shop. "How do you know her?"

"We met in the park on Halloween."

"Did she try to kill herself?"

"Yes. Luckily, her ex-boyfriend found her in time."

"And you randomly met him in New Orleans?"

"Yes. He told me why he left New York City and I realized that he was talking about the girl I met in the park."

"That's strange," said Alicia.

"Agreed," said Prince. "Today, you took me to the tea shop, and there she was. It's an amazing coincidence."

"Do you think she'll be okay?" asked Alicia.

"I hope so," said Prince. "She has so much more to explore in life."

"I can check in on her," said Alicia."I stop in sometimes to say hello to the manager."

"Thanks, Alicia," said Morgan.

~ 24 ~
Greenwich Village, New York City

A month after Mr. Bromwell's visit to the Charles Street Tavern, Steve Owens called the contact number on the back of the business card.

Three months after his call, Steve was back in New York City. He had accepted a part-time position with Ascenda Security. He was enrolled in a special program for returning students at NYU. He had moved into a dorm room on campus.

New age music played as Steve entered the Brewster Tea Shop in Greenwich Village in search of tea for study nights.

"Will that be all?" the clerk asked a customer at the counter.

Steve glanced up. He recognized the voice.

His ex-girlfriend stood behind the counter of the shop.

Steve browsed the aisles of the shop until he was the last customer. He stepped up to the counter with his tea.

"Ellen, hi," said Steve.

"Steve?" said Ellen. She lifted the hinged board over the counter and stepped out into the aisle. She hugged him.

"Thank you for coming to find me," she whispered. "You saved my life. "

"I'm still kicking myself for breaking up with you when I did," said Steve. "I knew that you'd be upset about turning thirty. I should have waited until after your birthday." He sighed.

"Steve, you have nothing to feel guilty about," said Ellen, shaking her head. "I'm the one who needs to apologize. I'm sorry for putting you through that."

"How are you doing, Ellen?"

"I'm good," she said. "Things are better. My therapist tells me that I'm on the upswing."

"Good."

"Steve, why are you here?" Ellen asked. "Last I knew, you were in New Orleans."

"I'm back in the city. I'm starting the fall term at NYU. I'm living in a dorm. Can you believe it?"

"Wow! Congratulations," said Ellen. "You're going to NYU? That's fantastic. How did it happen?"

"I had an amazing stroke of luck," said Steve. "A customer came into the bar one day and offered me a job that came with the chance to go to college here in New York. It's really unbelievable," he said. "I thought it was too good to be true, but here I am."

"That's fantastic. Congratulations, Steve," said Ellen. "I'm happy for you. You deserve good fortune."

~ 25 ~
Greenwich Village, New York City

Bells jingled, announcing the arrival of a customer at the Brewster Tea Shop in Greenwich Village. A man entered, sopping wet from the heavy rain outside, his hair dripping onto his summer-weight gray suit, his blue silk tie dripping from its edges. He wiped his face with a handkerchief.

"I should have carried an umbrella," he said.

"I'll get you a towel," said Ellen. She disappeared into the back room of the tea shop. Ellen returned with two towels.

"Thank you," said the man. He dried his hair with one towel. He used the other to try to sop up the water on his suit and tie.

"I wasn't expecting such a downpour," he said. "The good news is that my day is almost over."

Ellen glanced outside at the rain that continued to pour down. "Can I offer you a cup of tea while you wait for the rain to stop?" she asked.

"Thank you. That's very kind of you. I would enjoy that. The rain doesn't appear to be stopping anytime soon," he said. He smiled.

"Hello. I'm David Bromwell."

"Hi. I'm Ellen. What kind of tea would you like?"

"Can you recommend something?"

Ellen hesitated. "I really can't," she said. "My manager Neil usually makes recommendations but, unfortunately, he's not here this morning. He had to go to the DMV."

"Well, what varieties of oolong tea do you have?"

"Let me show you," said Ellen. She stepped out into the shop and led Mr. Bromwell to the barrels of tea. "We sell a lot of this one," she said, pointing to a barrel.

"Well, let's try it," said Mr. Bromwell.

"Okay." Ellen scooped some tea into a bag. "You can take a seat at a table in the back and I'll bring the tea out to you."

"Thank you, Ellen. Will you join me?" he asked. "Can we have a conversation?"

Ellen glanced around. The shop was empty. She nodded. "But I'll have to take care of any customers who come in."

"I understand perfectly."

New age music played softly from the overhead speakers as Ellen and Mr. Bromwell sipped the tea.

"I like it," said Ellen. "It's light but it has a nice flavor."

"A light flavor on a dark morning," said Mr. Bromwell. "Now you can recommend this one."

"I'll do that," said Ellen.

"How long have you worked here?"

"Only a few months," said Ellen. "Why? Do you think I should have learned the teas already?"

Mr. Bromwell smiled. "No. I wasn't thinking that at all."

"It's just that I want to do a good job," said Ellen. "This is the first job I've had in a while. I got fired from my last job. My manager Neil took a chance on me."

"How's it working out?"

"I like it here," said Ellen. "It's very peaceful. I get a lot of reading done between customers."

"It is a peaceful place," said Mr. Bromwell, nodding. "A refuge from the storm."

Ellen smiled.

"How long do you think you'll stay here?" Mr. Bromwell asked.

"I don't know," said Ellen. "It feels right for now. I guess I'll stay a while."

Mr. Bromwell nodded. He sipped his tea.

"Why did you get fired from your last job?"

"One day, I refused to pick pennies out of people's hands," said Ellen. "It wasn't my finest hour," she said, frowning. "I don't have that problem here. We have fewer customers and most pay with credit cards."

"I imagine that the new age music helps to soothe souls," said Mr. Bromwell.

Ellen nodded, smiling.

"Ellen, I'm always on the lookout for talent," said Mr. Bromwell. "I wonder if you would be interested in an opportunity with my firm." He pulled a card from the inside pocket of his suit jacket and handed it to her.

"What does 'AS' stand for?" asked Ellen.

"Ascenda Security," said Mr. Bromwell. "I manage a top-notch security outfit."

"I have no experience in security," said Ellen. "I barely have experience in tea," she said.

Mr. Bromwell smiled. "Ellen, I hire many agents across the globe," he said. "Sometimes, I meet a person and immediately get a sense that the person would be a good fit for the firm. I get that sense about you."

"Why? In what way?" said Ellen.

"Well, my business is often about connections," said

Mr. Bromwell. "The ability to make a connection can help an agent to gain information and assistance. Your offer of a cup of tea allowed us to connect."

The bells on the door of the tea shop jingled. Ellen's manager, Neil, dropped his umbrella into the stand near the door.

Ellen stood from the table.

"Hi. Neil. How was the DMV?"

"I had no idea that it would be so crowded, so early. I started reading the book you gave me while I was waiting. So far, I like it."

"I thought you would," said Ellen.

"Neil, this is Mr. Bromwell. He got caught in a downpour. I offered him a cup of tea. Mr. Bromwell, this is my manager, Neil," said Ellen.

"It's nice to meet you," said Neil, nodding. He lifted the hinged board on the counter. "I'm glad that I had my umbrella." Neil disappeared into the back room of the shop.

"I guess I should get back to work now," said Ellen.

Mr. Bromwell rose from the table.

"It was a pleasure meeting you, Ellen. Please keep my card. If you would consider a job change in the future, call the number on the back of my card."

Ellen squinted at the contact information.

"How long do I have to think about it?" asked Ellen.

Mr. Bromwell smiled.

"There is no time limit on my offer, Ellen," he said. "Take as much time as you need. Thank you for the conversation."

~ 26 ~

NYU Campus, New York City

Jamal led his friends up the stairs to his dorm room. He found his roommate sitting at his desk on the far side of the room.

"Right here, guys," said Jamal, pointing to the bed nearest the door. His friends unloaded their boxes on the floor. They exited the room to get another load.

"Wait for me, guys. I'll be right down."

Jamal picked up a green Jets football from the floor. He tossed it to his roommate.

"I guess we're roommates. I'm Jamal."

"Hi. I'm Steve. Sorry, dibs on the bed near the window."

"Yea, first come, first serve, and all that," said Jamal. "I would have done the same. When did you get here?"

"Yesterday."

"Beat me by a day," said Jamal. "Jets fan, huh?"

Steve nodded. He tossed the ball back to Jamal.

"I like the Giants," said Jamal.

"Where are you from?" Steve asked.

"Freeport, Long Island," said Jamal.

"I know where that is," said Steve.

"Where are you from?" Jamal asked.

"Here. New York," said Steve. "Though I was most recently living in New Orleans. It's an interesting place."

"I guess it is," said Jamal. "How long were you there?"

"About eight months," said Steve.

"You didn't like it?"

"New Orleans was okay," said Steve. "It was a good change for me. But I missed New York."

"Are you a freshman?" Jamal asked.

"Yes," said Steve. He laughed. "I know. I'm older than your average freshman. I took a few gap years."

Jamal tossed the ball back to Steve.

"It's nice to meet you, Steve," said Jamal. "I'd better go help my friends bring in the rest of my stuff."

Jamal read at his desk when Steve returned to the dorm room after midnight.

"Where are you coming from?" asked Jamal.

"I just got a job tending bar. I went in to ask about a job and the guy told me that if I could work the night, he'd hire me. So I did."

"How was it?"

"Slow," said Steve. "It's midweek."

"Wow, I'm not even old enough to drink in a bar," said Jamal. "It must be weird for you to be a student again."

"It is," said Steve. "But I'm thrilled to be here. I caught a lucky break."

"How?" asked Jamal.

"One afternoon, a customer came into the bar in New Orleans and offered me an opportunity to return to New York, work part-time for his firm, and go to college."

"Was he a regular customer?"

"No. I had never seen him before," said Steve.

"Why did he offer you the job?"

"He told me that he managed a security firm and he thought that I'd be well-suited to the field," said Steve. "He said that his business was saving lives and that I had demonstrated that commitment. "

"How?"

"He knew things about my past."

"Like what?"

"He knew the reason I was in New Orleans," said Steve.

"Why was that?" said Jamal.

Steve hesitated.

"I found my ex-girlfriend in her apartment on the night she tried to kill herself," said Steve. "Luckily, she survived."

"Your customer knew that?" said Jamal.

"Yes," said Steve. "And he knew that I had survived a fire at my house that had killed my parents."

"How did your customer know all that?" asked Jamal.

"I asked him the same question," said Steve. "He told me that he ran a state of the art security firm and that it was his business to know the background of potential employees."

"So, it wasn't random?" said Jamal. "He came into the bar to talk to you, specifically?"

"I guess he did," said Steve. "He left me his business card. About a month later, I called the contact number on the back of the card. Things happened quickly," he said. "I thought it was a scam, but here I am. He made it all happen."

~ 27 ~
New York City

Jamal raised his camera. He snapped a photograph of a young woman who leaned up against the wire fence of the basketball courts in Washington Square Park. Her hair was platinum, with streaks of pink and purple running through it. She wore jogging gear and garish orange sneakers. Jamal snapped a photo when she glanced up.

She held up her hand. "No."

Jamal lowered his camera. He walked across the lawn to her.

"Why are you photographing me?"

"I'm sorry to upset you," said Jamal. "I'm a photographer. I take pictures."

She shook her head. "My sister takes pictures," she said. "It can be very annoying."

"I respect that," said Jamal. "It's just that you caught my eye," he said. "You know, your pink and purple hair and those awful orange shoes."

She looked down at her brightly colored sneakers. "I guess they are ugly," she said. She chuckled. "I go through a lot of shoes."

"Hi. I'm Jamal."

"I'm Gwen. Do you live here or are you visiting?"

"I'm going to school here," said Jamal. "At NYU."

"Me, too," said Gwen. "Where are you from?"

"I'm from Freeport."

"I think that I've been there," said Gwen. "Are there a lot of fish restaurants along the water?"

"Yes. The Nautical Mile," said Jamal. "I worked in those restaurants for a few summers."

"My dad made me get a job in a diner here in the city for part of last summer," said Gwen. "I was terrible at it."

"It's hard work," said Jamal.

"Next summer, I'm going to try to get an internship," said Gwen. "Then my dad won't make me wait tables again."

"An internship?"

"Yes. I'm a math major," said Gwen. "Financial firms hire math majors for summer internships. Sometimes, they offer a job after graduation."

"That sounds good. Do you think that I would qualify for an internship?"

"Fine Arts?" Gwen shrugged. "I don't know. You should talk to your advisor."

"Thanks. I'll do that," said Jamal. "Well, now that we've properly met, can I take a few more photos of you?"

"You're just like Alicia," said Gwen, shaking her head.

"Show me your fierce side," said Jamal.

Gwen sneered.

"Show me your soft side."

"I don't have a soft side." Gwen laughed.

Jamal snapped a photo.

"Okay, that's enough." Gwen waved him away. "It's nice to meet you, Jamal. Maybe I'll see you on campus."

Gwen stepped in front of Jamal as he exited his calculus classroom.

"Jamal, hi," said Gwen. "Do you remember me?"

Jamal squinted at her. He looked down at her shoes.

"The girl with the orange shoes. Gwen, right?"

"Yes. Hi. I guess we're in the same calculus class."

"You're in Calc 1?"

"Yes. My dad suggested that familiar material might make it easier for me to settle into college," said Gwen.

"I see," said Jamal. "Well, I'm thinking that dropping this class might make it easier for me to settle into college. I can delay it until next semester."

"Don't drop it, Jamal. I can help you if you need it."

"I still have a few days to decide before registration closes," said Jamal. "I'll try the homework."

"Do you have another class right now?" asked Gwen.

"No. Not for two hours," said Jamal.

"Would you like to go for a cup of coffee?" she said. She held up a gift card. "It's a going-away gift from my Mom."

Gwen and Jamal watched the people coming and going from the subway station outside the Astor Coffeehouse.

"Where are you from?" Jamal asked.

"Here. Greenwich Village," said Gwen.

"Do you commute, since you live so close?"

"No. I live in a dorm," said Gwen. "My dad said he wants me to have the full college experience. He went here, too."

"It sounds like you and your dad are close."

"We are," said Gwen. "He's actually my stepfather."

"Are you in contact with your birth father?"

"I call him my ex-father," said Gwen. "We lost touch a few years ago. Though, recently, out of the blue, he contacted my mother and asked if my sister and I would meet with him."

"What did you say?"

"I haven't met with him," said Gwen. "My sister has."

"Aren't you curious?" said Jamal.

"Alicia tells me things."

"And that's enough for you?"

"Maybe," said Gwen. "I don't need two fathers."

"Maybe you need to tell him that."

Gwen frowned. "You think I should meet with him?"

"I don't know what you should do," said Jamal. "We just met."

"If it were your ex-father," said Gwen, "would you meet with him?"

"Yes," said Jamal.

"Is your father in your life?" asked Gwen.

"No. My father died when I was five," said Jamal.

"I'm sorry," said Gwen.

"Thank you," said Jamal. "So, if I had the opportunity to have my father back in my life again, even if only for five minutes," said Jamal, "I'd take it."

"Hmm," said Gwen. "I'll think about it."

~ 28 ~
Astor Coffeehouse, New York City

Morgan Prince joined his daughters at a table in the back of the Astor Coffeehouse.

"Hi. It's good to see you again, Alicia. Hi, Gwen. Thank you for coming," said Morgan.

Gwen nodded. "Hi."

"Morgan," said Alicia, "I got you a black coffee, dark roast. Is that okay?"

"That's perfect," said Morgan. He sipped the coffee. "That's good. Thanks."

Alicia smiled.

"What are you drinking?" asked Morgan.

"I'm drinking hot chocolate," said Alicia. "Now that Gwen's in college, she drinks chai tea." Alicia rolled her eyes.

Gwen shook her head at her sister. "Alicia, I drank chai tea in high school," she said.

"I never saw you drink it," said Alicia.

"Because you were never with me," said Gwen.

"Gwen," said Morgan, "congratulations on gaining acceptance to NYU. That's an impressive accomplishment. How's it going?"

“Well, it’s still early in the semester but I like it.”

“You’ll learn so much there,” said Morgan. “You’ll have opportunities that can take you around the world.”

Gwen nodded. “That’s what my dad says.” She glanced down at her phone.

“Your dad’s right,” said Morgan. “College is a special experience. I hope that you enjoy every bit of your time there.”

Gwen nodded.

“Thanks.” She sipped her tea. She texted a message to Jamal.

‘In coffeehouse with ex-father.’

“Morgan, do you want to come to my violin recital next month?” asked Alicia.

“Why don’t you have your mom send me the information?” said Prince. “My schedule can be somewhat erratic,” he said, “but I’ll check to see if I’ll can make it.”

“Okay,” said Alicia. She typed a message on her phone to her mother.

“Morgan, do you still live in San Diego?” asked Gwen.

“I live nearby, in La Jolla,” said Prince.

“Posh,” whispered Alicia.

Gwen frowned at her sister.

“Alicia, tell us something good that happened for you this week,” said Morgan.

“My ice hockey team beat Millcrest Academy and I scored a goal,” said Alicia. “Yay!”

“Congratulations!” said Morgan. “Ice hockey is a tough sport.”

“I told her that she should stop playing,” said Gwen. “She’s already had two concussions.”

“I like it,” said Alicia. “It’s fun.” Alicia shrugged. “Gwen takes kick boxing at college.”

“I just started it, but I like it,” said Gwen.

"Kick boxing is an excellent skill," said Morgan. "It's come in handy for me, from time to time. I'd encourage you to stick with it."

Gwen nodded. She squinted at Morgan.

"Are you dying?" she asked.

"I told you," said Alicia.

"No, I'm not dying. Why did you ask me that?"

"Well, why did you reach out to us now?" asked Gwen.

"I realized that I made a terrible mistake by losing contact with the two of you," said Prince. "It took me a long time to realize it." He shook his head.

"I'm not dying," said Morgan. "I reached out because I wanted to reestablish communication with the two of you."

"Why did you drop us?" said Gwen.

Prince shook his head.

"I can't give any good reason to justify it," he said. "You girls were growing up and it was hard to stay up-to-date with you from such a distance. I just let more and more time elapse between our calls until we had no contact at all. I'm sorry," he said. "It was a big mistake."

"Dan's our Dad now," said Gwen.

"Yes," said Morgan. "I know that. I have no intention of disrupting your family. I'd just like to try to reestablish a relationship with the two of you, if that's possible."

"As our ex-father?" said Gwen.

"That works," said Morgan.

Alicia smiled.

"Well, I'm pretty busy at school," said Gwen. "I don't know how often I'll be able to meet."

"It's true," said Alicia. "Mom says that now that Gwen is in college, she can hardly get in touch with her anymore."

Gwen frowned at Alicia.

"Well, I still travel frequently for work," said Morgan,

"so I'm not sure how frequently I'll get to New York. I told your mother I'll reach out whenever it looks like I'll be in proximity of the city. If either of you is available, we can meet."

"And, do what?" said Gwen. "Talk?"

"Well, I hope we'll talk," said Morgan.

Alicia smiled.

"Gwen, tell us something good that happened for you since you went to college," said Prince.

"I made a friend," said Gwen.

Jamal spotted Gwen in the back of the Astor Coffeehouse. He purchased a cup of coffee and carried it to her table.

"Hi, Gwen," said Jamal.

"Jamal, hi." Gwen stood to greet him.

"Morgan and Alicia," said Gwen, "this is my friend Jamal, from NYU. We're both freshman. Jamal, this is my sister, Alicia. And this is my birth father, Morgan Prince."

"Hi, Alicia," said Jamal. "Gwen says that you're a photographer. Is that right?"

Alicia smiled. She nodded.

Morgan stood to shake Jamal's hand.

"Hello, Jamal," he said.

"Hello, Mr. Prince," he said.

Jamal glanced at Gwen. He stared at Prince.

"Mr. Prince, I think that we've met before."

"We have?" said Prince.

"You have?" said Gwen. "When?"

"Mr. Prince, I believe that we were seat mates on a flight to Florida," said Jamal. "I sat in the window seat."

"Ah, I see," said Prince. "I'm not sure that we formally met on the plane," he said.

"I sat next to Samantha," said Jamal. "What a coincidence to run into you again," he said. "And to find out that you're Gwen's father." Jamal shook his head.

"How is it possible that you've met before?" said Gwen.

Alicia laughed.

"Well, I suppose that coincidences happen more often than we expect," said Prince.

"How often do we expect them?" said Gwen.

"Oh, no. Don't get her started," said Alicia. "She's a math major."

"Mr. Prince," said Jamal, "have you been in contact with Samantha since the flight?"

"I ran into her in New Orleans in the spring," said Prince.

"I ran into her in Dallas, in the spring," said Jamal.

"She mentioned that she ran into you in Dallas," said Prince. "She said that you helped her."

"My friend and I tackled a guy," said Jamal, shrugging.

"Samantha was appreciative of that," said Morgan.

"I saw her on New Year's Eve, too," said Jamal.

Morgan nodded. "She told me that, too."

"It's crazy that you two have already met," said Gwen.

Jamal nodded. "Well, I'm headed to my study group. Gwen, are you coming tonight?"

"Hmm. Probably not," said Gwen. "I'll walk you out."

"Alicia," said Jamal, "it was nice to meet you. Mr. Prince, it was good to see you again."

Gwen walked Jamal to the door of the coffeehouse.

"Thanks for coming to save me," said Gwen.

"I figured I'd give you an excuse to leave, if you wanted."

Gwen glanced back at Morgan. "I guess he's okay," she said. "Maybe a little boring." She shook her head. "But I can't believe that you already met him. That's just weird."

~ 29 ~
Jones Beach, New York

Samantha parked in the Field 6 lot at Jones Beach. It was the off-season and there were only about fifteen cars in the lot. Per the message on her device, Samantha parked and walked up to the boardwalk.

Though it was the off-season, people braved the autumn chill to walk west on the two-mile boardwalk path. Samantha heard laughter in the opposite direction. A group of men stood together laughing outside the Jones Beach Cafeteria.

As Samantha approached, one of the men in her path bowed, and held the door to the cafeteria open for her.

Inside the cafeteria, two employees, a cashier and a cook, manned the concession counter. Samantha purchased a cup of coffee and took it to an empty table in the middle of the room. Only three other tables were occupied.

A family of four sat at the table nearest Samantha, to her right. The children stared down at their phones.

A woman and two young children chattered in Spanish at a table near the ocean side entrance to the building.

A man sat alone at a table near the northern entrance to the cafeteria. His black baseball cap hid his face. He stared down at his phone.

The door on the southern side of the cafeteria opened, carrying the men's laughter into the room. Two teenagers entered, talking loudly.

The man in the baseball cap looked up at them.

Samantha saw his face.

She felt a prickle of fear.

The man sitting in the Jones Beach Cafeteria was the same man from the Bourbon Street Café in New Orleans. He was the same man who had winked at Samantha as he had exited the New Orleans bar with the woman in the sparkling red dress.

Samantha pushed her hair up into her hat and put on her sunglasses. She exited the cafeteria on the southern side of the building, walking hurriedly past the group of men standing outside.

Samantha created a diagram of the Field 6 parking lot. She drove through the lot, stopping at each parked vehicle to record its location, make, model, and license plate number. She captured any notable features.

A yellow low-rider parked behind the cafeteria had horizontal black stripes on each side.

A red Ford truck had rusted through on the bottom.

The bed of a black Dodge Ram was covered with a black tonneau. The truck had a broken taillight on its right side.

Samantha drove back to the western end of the lot and parked. She turned off the car's engine. She checked her device. She had no new messages. She sat in her car and waited.

The sun began its descent in the sky and people came off the boardwalk to claim their vehicles in the lot.

Samantha crossed off their cars on her diagram.

The cafeteria closed for the day It began to empty.

The family of four climbed into a green Nissan Pathfinder parked near the entrance to the boardwalk.

The woman and the two children climbed into a white Kia Optima.

The group of men scattered across the lot. One of the men got into the rusted red Ford truck.

The man in the black baseball cap walked into view on the ocean side of the cafeteria. He walked west on the boardwalk.

The cashier and the cook exited the cafeteria together.

The cook climbed into the yellow low-rider.

The cashier claimed a silver Honda Civic that was parked two spaces to the left of the low-rider.

There was one vehicle remaining in the lot, the black Dodge Ram. As the skies darkened, the man in the black baseball cap came off the boardwalk and claimed it.

Samantha sank down into her seat. She heard the Ram truck's engine revving. She heard the truck accelerate as the driver steered it to the exit on the eastern end of the lot.

Samantha peered through her driver's window to see the truck pull out of the lot and onto the eastbound lanes of Ocean Parkway. Samantha followed. She pulled her car onto the eastbound lanes of Ocean Parkway. She tracked the Dodge Ram ahead of her by the white bulb in the broken taillight. She maintained her distance as she followed.

The brake lights flashed on the Dodge Ram. The truck stopped in the roadway.

Samantha pulled her car to the side of the road.

The truck pulled off the roadway.

Samantha waited for the Ram to reappear.

When it did, the driver sped east on Ocean Parkway.

Samantha drove slowly on Ocean Parkway, scanning

for the area where the Ram had pulled off the roadway.

She saw a sandy trail that led over the dunes to the ocean. A sign warned that the area was for use by emergency vehicles only. A rusted chain lay on the ground between two concrete posts.

Samantha pulled her car off the roadway. She parked and walked through the concrete posts to the top of the dune. She entered the vegetation to the east of the path.

Brambles scratched Samantha's face as she pushed through the wild vegetation. About twenty five feet in, she saw the roll of carpeting lying on the ground amidst the brush. She approached.

She dialed 911.

Samantha gave the dispatcher the latitude and longitude of her location. She gave a description of the Dodge Ram, and it's license plate number. Samantha noted that the truck had a broken taillight on its right side.

A reporter from Channel Eight News stood against the backdrop of the dunes on the southern side of Ocean Parkway. The reporter's hair blew in the afternoon breeze.

"Suffolk County police discovered the body of a local college student in the dunes behind me last night," said the reporter. "The victim has been identified as Lucy Cobb, a sophomore at Adelphi University. Ms. Cobb was reported missing by her college roommate when she failed to return to school last weekend," said the reporter.

"Police credit an observant witness for the arrest of a suspect in the case. Police tell us that evidence at the crime scene matches evidence found in the suspect's truck."

The reporter from Channel Eight News stood in front of the dunes on Ocean Parkway. Her hair blew in the afternoon breeze.

"Preliminary DNA testing suggests that the suspect arrested in the murder of an Adelphi College student whose body was found here on Jones Beach may be linked to two other unsolved murders earlier this year," said the reporter.

"The two victims in the unsolved cases were found in New Orleans."

~ 30 ~
Baltimore, Maryland

Jake Watson sat in his jail cell, his eyes closed. Every day that he had been behind bars for the assault on Ceci Torres, Jake had searched for his missing wife Melissa and his daughter Janie.

After months of searching, a private investigator he had hired revealed that Jake's wife and daughter were living in Baltimore, under the names Melody and Alice Quinn.

Finally, Jake had his answer to the puzzle over what had happened to his family. His wife hadn't been abducted or murdered. She had left him, plain and simple, as he had suspected. She had tried to escape him. His wife had dared to take his daughter away from him.

Jake took a deep breath and let it out slowly, a technique he had learned from his mandated anger management sessions. He breathed in. He breathed out.

He couldn't let it stand.

Since accepting a part-time position with Ascenda Security, Harry Quigley's jobs had all been local to New Jersey. He saw a job posting in Baltimore and accepted the assignment. Harry had fond memories of Baltimore. He and his late wife Edith had enjoyed many weekends at the Inner Harbor. Harry was able to take Jesse with him on the job.

From Monday to Friday of the week, Harry was tasked with patrolling in front of the Canton Elementary School as the children were released to the buses at the end of the school day.

On Friday, the last day of his assignment, Harry once again guided Jesse along the sidewalk in front of the Canton Elementary School. Harry noticed the last car parked in the driveway. It was a black Ford Explorer with New York plates.

Harry held Jesse back as the driver of the Ford Explorer carelessly backed out of the driveway in front of them and sped up the road. Harry reported the vehicle's license plate number to the firm.

Melissa Watson was frantic.

Janie hadn't gotten off the school bus. She paced at the bus stop while she waited for the police to arrive.

Melissa replayed recent incidents in her head.

Janie's teacher had contacted Melissa to tell her that Janie had signed her class artwork as Janie, not Alice, and had burst into tears when the teacher asked her about it. Could that have been enough for Jake to find them?

Melissa and Janie had returned with groceries one Saturday afternoon to see a black sedan parked on the street. The driver of the vehicle had hidden his face behind a newspaper. Melissa had hurriedly ushered Janie past the car.

Melissa heard sirens in the distance. She grew more frantic. She sent a message.

'Janie didn't get off the school bus.'

The reply came quickly.

'Lila's on it.'

Jamal and Gwen sat in the dining room of the Maryland House on I-95. The two had driven to Baltimore for a photography exhibition on Friday morning and had stopped to eat before their return to New York City. The rest area buzzed with activity as people got a jump on their weekend plans.

"Thanks for coming with me today," said Jamal. "And thanks for lending your car. I was going to take the train."

"You're welcome," said Gwen. "My car mostly just sits in the garage. I guess it's good for it to get some use once in a while. Today was fun. It was an early start to the day," she said, "but still fun."

A foursome entered the dining area. Two men who looked enough alike to be brothers claimed a booth at the back of the room. The woman with them lifted a young girl into the booth. The girl wailed. The men left to purchase food. The girl attempted to escape the woman by climbing on top of the table.

The men returned with two trays of food.

The woman placed a hot dog and a carton of milk in front of the girl. The girl wailed. The woman pulled the girl out of the booth, and through the dining area, to the hallway that led to the ladies' room.

Jamal and Gwen tossed their trash and stowed their trays. They entered the corridor leading to the bathrooms.

Jamal waited for Gwen in the hallway outside the rest rooms. He recognized a woman who entered the rest area.

"Samantha?" he said, stepping alongside her.

"Jamal? What are you doing here?" asked Samantha.

The two moved out of the line of traffic.

"My friend and I went to Baltimore for a photo exhibition," said Jamal. "We're on our way back to school. Why are you here?"

"I'm working. I'm looking for an abducted girl."

Jamal squinted at her.

"Well, I don't know if it's her," said Jamal, "but two men and a woman came in with a girl a little while ago. The girl's been screaming ever since. The woman took her into the bathroom. My friend is in there."

"Your friend's in the bathroom?"

"Yes," said Jamal. "Her name is Gwen. She has pink and purple hair."

"Okay. Thanks, Jamal."

Samantha disappeared into the ladies' room.

Samantha stood in front of a sink next to the girl with pink and purple hair. Samantha stared into the mirror at the woman who leaned against the first bathroom stall.

The woman knocked gently on the stall door.

"How's it going in there, Hon?" said the woman.

The girl didn't answer.

"Hurry up," said the woman. "We can bring the food to the car, if you want. You can eat it there, then go back to sleep."

"No!" wailed the girl.

"Hurry up!" said the woman. "Johnny's waiting for us."

The girl wailed.

The woman stepped out of the corridor of bathroom stalls. She stood in front of the last sink in the room and arranged her hair in the mirror. She leaned over to apply lipstick.

Samantha lunged at the woman, knocking her sideways into the wall at the end of the bank of sinks. The woman's lipstick clattered to the floor.

The women at the sinks gasped.

The woman scrambled to her feet. She kicked out at Samantha.

Samantha blocked her kick. She kicked out at the woman, knocking her back against the bathroom wall. The woman stayed down.

The women at the sinks scattered.

"Gwen?" said Samantha, to the girl with pink and purple hair. "Tell Jamal to get help!"

Samantha knocked softly on the door to the first stall.

"Little girl," she said, "you can come out now. You're safe. Let's get you back to your mother."

The girl unlatched the stall door. She stared out, tears streaming down her face.

Samantha reached for her.

"Everything's going to be okay," she said. She squinted at the girl.

Samantha recognized her.

"Are you Janie?" she whispered in the girl's ear.

"No! I'm Alice!" The girl wailed.

"It's okay, Alice," Samantha whispered. "You're safe now."

Samantha helped Janie into the police car waiting at the curb.

"Samantha?"

Jamal stood with Gwen on the sidewalk.

"I just wanted to introduce you formally to my friend," he said. "Samantha, this is Gwen Prince. We go to NYU together. Gwen, this is Samantha. We met on a plane."

Gwen squinted at Jamal. "On the same flight where you met Morgan?"

"Yes," said Jamal. "Samantha, Gwen is Mr. Prince's daughter. Gwen recently introduced him to me."

"You're Morgan's daughter?" said Samantha. "Wow. What a surprise to meet you. Thank you for helping me today."

"I didn't do anything," said Gwen, shrugging. "You're really good at kick boxing."

"I've had a lot of training."

"Morgan's been trained in kick boxing, too," said Gwen.

"It's an excellent skill," said Samantha.

"That's what he said."

An officer tapped on the hood of the police car.

"Are you ready to go, Ma'am?"

"Yes, Officer," said Samantha.

"Jamal, it was good to see you again. Gwen, it's a pleasure to meet you. Thank you both for helping me today," she said. "Have a good trip back to New York."

Samantha waved and got into the police car next to Janie.

The police car pulled away from the curb.

Samantha typed a message to Morgan.

'I met your daughter Gwen in Baltimore! With Jamal!'

~ 31 ~

Baltimore, Maryland

Morgan Prince stood in the shadow of a cement column across the street from a narrow three-story brick apartment building in Baltimore. The only lights in the building came from the apartment on the second floor. Prince reread the message on his device.

'Apartment B. Take Melissa Watson, aka Melody Quinn, to safety.'

Prince crossed the street. He held his wrist device up to the electronic reader at the entrance to the building and was buzzed through to the small lobby. He took the stairs to the second floor. Prince knocked lightly on the door of Apartment B.

There was no response. He knocked again.

"Mrs. Quinn," said Prince. "My name is Morgan Prince. I'm here to help you."

"I've already spoken to the police," said the voice behind the door.

"I'm not the police. I'm a security agent. I'm here to protect you."

"My daughter is the one who needs help. She didn't get off the bus today."

"Mrs. Quinn, I'm sorry about your daughter. I wasn't aware that she was missing. I hope that she'll be found soon," said Prince. "But I'm here to protect you. You're also in danger."

"Who sent you?" Melissa whispered.

Prince's device buzzed with a new message. He squinted at the message on his wrist device.

"Lila," he said.

"Lila? Jake found us?" Melissa gasped. "Did Jake take Janie?"

"Mrs. Quinn, I only know that I need to take you to safety right now. Will you come with me?"

Melissa unlocked the door. She peered at Prince through the opening in the chain lock.

Prince and Melissa boarded the freight elevator at the end of the hallway. They exited from the basement into an alleyway behind the building.

A white Honda CR-V was parked near the door.

Prince drove the vehicle to the end of the alleyway.

The device on his wrist buzzed.

'Daughter safe, at Baltimore Medical.'

Prince waited outside the hospital for Melissa to emerge with her daughter.

His wrist device buzzed.

'Escort client to Sunbird Cab. Pursue suspect at client's apartment building.'

Prince saw the cab parked down the street. Its light was off. He approached the driver's side of the vehicle and knocked on the window.

The driver rolled his window down part way.

"Are you taking passengers?" asked Prince.

"No. I'm waiting for someone," said the driver.

"A woman and her daughter?"

"Yes. Are you her escort?"

"Yes," said Prince. "I expect she'll be out soon."

Prince squinted at the driver.

"Steve?" he said. "Is that you?"

The driver of the cab squinted back at him.

"Mr. Prince? From New Orleans?"

"Yes. What are you doing here? You're driving a cab? Do you live in Baltimore now?"

"No, Mr. Prince," said Steve. "I'm back in New York City. I'm working and I started the fall term at NYU. I'm in a work/study program. This is my first job assignment."

"What kind of work is it?" Prince asked.

"I do odd jobs for a security company."

"Security?" repeated Prince. "Huh. What firm?"

"Ascenda Security. Have you heard of it?"

Prince squinted at Steve. "Yes, I have."

Prince tapped the screen of his wrist device. The Ascenda Security logo filled the screen. He held up the device for Steve to see.

"I also work for Ascenda," said Prince.

"You do? Were you working for Ascenda when I met you in New Orleans?"

"Yes. I was," said Prince.

"Wow, what a coincidence," said Steve.

"Yes," said Prince. "Who hired you?"

"Mr. David Bromwell," said Steve. "Do you know him?"

"Yes. I do," said Prince. "How did you meet him?"

"He came into the bar about a month after I met you," said Steve. "Mr. Bromwell offered me a part-time job and help going to college in New York. He got me into a special program for returning students at NYU. He made it all happen, just like he said he would. It's amazing," said Steve.

"Well, I guess that makes us colleagues," said Prince. "Welcome aboard."

"Thank you, Mr. Prince."

Prince ushered Melissa and Janie into the back seat of the Sunbird Cab.

"It seems that I've been reassigned," said Prince. "Steve will help you the rest of the way. You're in good hands. Best wishes to you and your daughter."

Prince closed the door of the cab. He waved.

Steve pulled the car away from the curb.

Steve parked the Sunbird Cab next to a black stretch limousine in the far corner of the parking lot of the Maryland House. He ushered Melissa and her daughter out of the cab and into the back seat of the limousine.

A man wearing a crisp gray suit and a burgundy tie sat on the seat across from them.

"Will that be all, sir?" asked Steve.

"Yes, that's it for tonight, Steve. Thank you. Have a good trip back to New York."

"Thank you, Mr. Bromwell. Good luck, Ma'am." Steve closed the door to the limousine.

Mr. Bromwell smiled at Melissa.

"Can we have a conversation?" he asked.

Melissa Watson pulled out of the parking lot of the Maryland House in a black Hyundai Santa Fe, and drove north to the New Jersey Turnpike. Janie slept in the back seat.

Melissa listened to a news broadcast on the car radio.

"Four suspects have been arrested in an abduction and murder plot involving a local woman and her daughter. All four suspects have implicated the woman's husband, Mr. Jake Watson, as the mastermind behind the plot. Mr. Watson is in prison for an unrelated conviction."

Melissa switched off the radio.

She frowned.

She knew that Jake would never give up searching for them. She and Janie would have to start again, in a new place, under new names. It would be hard on Janie. She sighed.

Melissa drove north on I-95 to the New Jersey Turnpike. She took Exit 6 on the Turnpike and drove west into Pennsylvania.

~ 32 ~

Marlton, New Jersey

Samantha sipped a milkshake in Olga's Diner in Marlton, New Jersey. She glanced into the mirror behind the counter as people entered and left the diner. She stared into the mirror as a man entered and took a booth along the windows.

Samantha carried her milkshake to the man's table.

"I'd recommend a vanilla milkshake," she said.

Morgan Prince glanced up at her.

"Samantha?" He stood from the booth to greet her. "What are you doing here?" he asked.

"I finished a job in Baltimore and was headed north," she said. "The guide suggested that Olga's was a good place to stop along the way."

"Ah," said Morgan. "I also came from Baltimore. What good fortune to run into you here. Would you like to join me?"

Samantha slid into the seat across from him. "Did you get my message?" she asked.

"No, I didn't," said Prince. "My phone's been off all night." He pulled the phone from his pocket and powered it on.

The server arrived to take Prince's order.

"I'll have a vanilla milkshake," said Prince.

He read Samantha's message on his phone.

"You met Gwen?"

"Yes," said Samantha. "She was with Jamal at the Maryland House on I-95. It seems that they're friends at school. How amazing is that?"

"I recently learned that myself," said Prince. "I met Gwen and Alicia in a coffeehouse near the NYU campus. At our first meeting, Gwen introduced me to her friend Jamal. She was shocked that we had already met."

"What are the odds?" said Samantha.

The served delivered Prince's milkshake.

"When I saw Gwen in Baltimore, she mentioned that you had commented on kick boxing. So, I assumed that you were in touch again. I'm happy for you," said Samantha.

"Well, we've met once," said Prince. "I'm not sure that she'll agree to meet with me again," he said, "but I loved seeing her," he said.

"Why were Jamal and Gwen at the Maryland House?"

"They were returning from a photo exhibition in Baltimore," said Samantha.

"Why were you there?" Prince asked.

"I was working. I went to check the ladies' room for an abducted girl, and there was Jamal. He told me that he was waiting for his friend Gwen who was in the bathroom. I found the girl in the bathroom and asked Gwen to tell Jamal to get help."

"How did you know it was her?" Prince asked.

"Jamal told me that his friend had pink and purple hair."

"That's Gwen," said Prince.

"Jamal formally introduced her to me before I left the Maryland House with the abducted girl," said Samantha. "He introduced her to me as his friend, Gwen Prince, Mr. Prince's daughter. Imagine my surprise," she said.

"Jamal has now shown up on two of my jobs," said Samantha. "first in Dallas, and now in Baltimore. It's strange. And meeting Gwen, and finding out that she's Jamal's friend, and your daughter, is even stranger." Samantha shook her head.

"I agree," said Prince. "Worlds collide."

The two sipped their shakes.

"I knew the girl on the job in Baltimore," said Samantha. "I helped her mother escape her husband back some time ago, in New Jersey. I took the girl to Baltimore Medical to be reunited with her mother. I've helped her twice now."

"I think we were assigned to the same case," said Prince. "I protected a woman from a killer hired by her husband. I took the woman to Baltimore Medical to be reunited with her daughter."

"When I helped her leave her husband," said Samantha, "she told me that, if her husband found her, he'd kill her."

"It seems he tried," said Prince. "He sent someone to her apartment to kill her."

"That makes three times that she's been helped."

"I guess the firm's protection continues until the client's safe," said Morgan.

"Do you think that she's safe now?" asked Samantha.

"I assume that she is," said Prince. "After her daughter was released to her, I escorted her to a cab parked on the street," he said. "I knew the cab driver. Do you remember I told you about Steve in New Orleans? He saved Ellen, the girl I met in the park on Halloween?"

"Yes, I remember," said Samantha. "You prevented him from being mugged, right?"

"Yes," said Prince. "Well, Steve was the cab driver. Imagine my surprise," he said.

"Was he just some random cab driver?"

"No. Not at all," said Prince. "He works part-time for

Ascenda Security."

"How did that happen?" asked Samantha.

"It seems that, about a month after I met Steve in New Orleans, Mr. Bromwell paid him a visit. He offered Steve an opportunity to return to New York and go to college while working part-time for the firm."

"Do you think that Steve was offered the job because he saved Ellen?"

"Maybe," said Prince.

"Hmm," said Samantha. "You said that it was odd for you to be assigned to prevent a mugging. Maybe that wasn't the real job," she said.

"Maybe you're an advance man," said Samantha. "A recruiter. You met with Steve and then he was hired by Mr. Bromwell. Just like I was."

Prince squinted at Samantha. He shrugged.

The two sipped their milkshakes.

"Morgan, do you remember me talking about the couple in the bar on Bourbon Street in New Orleans?"

"The woman in the sparkling red dress?"

"Yes," said Samantha. "Last month, I had a job at Jones Beach, in New York, and that same guy was there. He dumped a body in the brush off the beach. I gave the police the license plate number of his truck and they caught him. It turns out that he's a serial killer. His DNA is a match to two unsolved murders in New Orleans."

Samantha frowned, shaking her head.

"I keep thinking that the woman in the red dress is one of his victims. I had a bad feeling about the guy that night but I failed to protect her. I should have acted. Maybe I could have saved a life."

"But you don't know for sure that she's one of his victims," said Prince.

"No, I don't," said Samantha. "Even so, I should have done more to help her."

Prince nodded. "That's how I felt about Ellen on Halloween. She was sad. I should have done more to help her."

"From now on," said Samantha, "if I see someone who needs help, I'm going to act, even if I'm not assigned to them."

~ 33 ~
New Jersey

Harry Quigley slid into the seat across from Ceci Torres at Lola's Restaurant in Englewood Cliffs.

"Hi, Ceci. How are you feeling? You look great."

"I'm feeling pretty good, Harry," she said. "I feel like I finally have my life back."

"Jesse's ears perked up when I told him I was having lunch with you today."

Ceci smiled. "Well, give him an extra biscuit from me," she said. "How are things at the Paramus Gardens?"

"Quiet, said Harry. "Your apartment is still vacant. Where is Denise living?"

"She's sharing a house in Queens with six other flight attendants who are based out of JFK."

"What a life she has," said Harry. "She must love to travel."

"She does," said Ceci.

"Where are you living?"

"In New Brunswick," said Ceci. "I came up last night to visit my parents."

"How are they doing?" asked Harry.

"Good. They're still watching over me."

"You're their daughter," said Harry. "How is life in New Brunswick?"

"It's good. I share a house with three roommates near the Rutgers Campus. I'm working two jobs again. I tend bar and I work at a gym downtown. I'm auditing a class at Rutgers. I'm even thinking about applying for next year."

"That's wonderful," said Harry. "It sounds like you have your energy back."

"I do," said Ceci. "I feel reborn." She smiled.

"I'm glad to hear it, Ceci."

"What's new with you, Harry?"

"Guess what? I'm working again," said Harry.

"You are? What are you doing?"

"I work part-time for a security firm," said Harry. "A man came by the apartment one afternoon and told me that he could use my observation skills in his firm. I work a few hours a week, mostly local jobs. It suits me."

Harry and Ceci parted outside Lola's Restaurant. Harry waved as Ceci walked down the block to retrieve her car.

Two women pushed baby strollers across the intersection. One woman opened the driver's door to a car parked at the curb. The other woman crossed the street to her SUV parked near the corner of the intersection. The woman lifted her baby into the car's infant seat. She stored the stroller in the back of the vehicle. She climbed into the driver's seat and started the engine.

The woman opened the driver's door and got out of the vehicle. She held a cookie tin in her hand. She left the car running and crossed back over the street to her friend who was still parked at the curb.

The woman handed the cookie tin to the driver of the vehicle. She waved as her friend pulled away.

The woman waited for the light to change to cross back over the street to her vehicle. As she waited, a man climbed into the driver's seat of her car.

"No!" the woman shouted. She ignored the blaring car horns as she crossed against the light.

"No! My baby!" she yelled. "My baby! My baby!"

The vehicle pulled away from the curb. The driver turned at the corner and disappeared down the road.

Harry Quigley sent the vehicle's license plate number to the firm.

Samantha's device buzzed.

'Rescue baby at Branch Brook Park, Newark.'

Samantha arrived at the park in the early autumn chill and searched for the missing baby.

She walked through the brush around the parking lot.

She walked the pathways of the park.

She checked the trash bins.

She searched the brush behind the tennis courts.

Samantha heard the cries of an infant.

She saw a bit of blue poking out of the brush. She found the baby wrapped in a blue blanket.

She dialed 911.

Samantha's device buzzed again. She read the new message.

'Times Square Subway Station, #1 Train South.'

~ 34 ~

Bryant Park, New York City

Jamal aimed his camera at the people sitting in randomly positioned folding chairs on the Bryant Park lawn. He took photos of the commuters who hurriedly cut through the park to get to Sixth Avenue. Jamal aimed his camera at a man sitting alone at the edge of the treeline.

The man sat in a chair, facing in Jamal's direction. He wore a long black overcoat, black sunglasses, and a black fedora on his head. His legs were crossed elegantly at the knee, his black dress shoes shiny in the late afternoon sun.

Jamal took a few photographs. He walked closer to the man and changed his angle. He raised his camera.

The man held up his hand. He shook his head.

Jamal lowered his camera.

The man beckoned to him.

"Hello, sir," said Jamal.

"What's your name?"

"Jamal Williams, sir."

"Well, Jamal, I don't mean to be unfriendly," said the man, "but I'd prefer not to have my photograph taken unless I commission it."

"I understand," said Jamal. "My apologies. I'll delete them." He tapped on the camera screen.

"Okay, sir, they're gone," he said, nodding. "Have a good evening, sir."

Jamal left the park.

He walked behind the rush of commuters heading home for the evening. He followed the crowd to the Times Square subway station.

Jamal zipped his camera into its case and packed it away into his backpack. He headed for the #1 Train South.

~ 35 ~
New York City

The southbound #1 and #2 trains at Times Square were running late. Tempers flared as the crowd swelled on the platform.

Samantha Baker stood in the alcove near the elevator to avoid being jostled by the crowd.

The subway train's headlights appeared down the track.

The crowd surged forward.

A woman screamed.

The woman charged through the crowd, swinging a toy sword at anyone in her path. She uttered a stream of gibberish as she swung the sword.

Samantha pushed through the crowd to follow the woman.

Commuters stepped aside to avoid being struck by the woman's sword. An aisle opened between the parted crowd, leading to the edge of the platform. There, a girl in a plaid school uniform listened to music on her headphones, oblivious to the woman with the sword.

The woman swung, hitting the violin case that hung from the girl's back. She swung again.

The girl screamed. She fell onto the tracks below.

Commuters on the platform echoed her screams.

The woman with the sword changed direction, swinging her sword through the crowd to make an exit.

Samantha reached the edge of the platform.

The girl stood below her on the tracks. The girl removed her violin case from her back and tossed it toward the platform. She took a step forward.

The train conductor blasted a warning.

"No! Get down!" Samantha yelled.

The girl stood, frozen, on the tracks, staring at the headlights of the oncoming train.

The engineer blasted another warning.

Samantha jumped off the platform. She pushed the girl forward.

"Into the drainage ditch!" Samantha yelled. "Stay down! The train will roll over us. Don't move! Stay down!"

The train rumbled into the station, its brakes squealing, as it rolled over them. The engineer stopped the train in the tunnel down the tracks.

Samantha moved to the girl's side.

"Are you okay?" she asked.

The girl stared at the pieces of her violin case that were scattered along the tracks. Strings from her violin hung from a concrete beam.

"I'm okay. Thank you. I didn't know what to do."

"What's your name?" Samantha asked.

"Alicia."

"Hi, Alicia. I'm Samantha. Does anything hurt?"

"I think I sprained my left ankle. Maybe my wrist."

"Let's get you some help," said Samantha. She helped Alicia up from the tracks. She supported her as they stepped to the platform.

Jamal arrived on the #1 train platform as commuters lifted the girl up to safety and circled her on the platform. He joined the commuters who offered a hand to the woman who still stood on the tracks.

Samantha waved them away.

"Please help the girl," she said. "I'll use the ladder down the track. Thank you."

Jamal stared down at her.

"Samantha?"

"Jamal? What are you doing here?"

"I'm headed back to campus," said Jamal. "What happened? Are you okay?"

"I'm fine, Jamal," said Samantha. "A woman pushed a girl off the platform with a toy sword. Would you make sure that she gets help?"

"Okay," said Jamal. "Are you sure you're okay?"

"Yes. Thank you, Jamal."

Samantha walked down the track to the ladder.

Jamal joined the circle of commuters surrounding the girl. She sat on the platform in her plaid school uniform.

Jamal squinted at her.

"Alicia?" he asked.

Alicia looked up at him. "Hi, Jamal. What are you doing here?"

"I was taking pictures. Are you okay?" Jamal asked.

"I'm okay. I think I have a sprained ankle and a sprained wrist but I've had worse injuries with ice hockey."

A garbled voice came over the subway speakers.

"Passengers, this station is closed due to a police investigation. Please use alternate routes for your commute home tonight."

A groan rose from the crowd on the platform. The commuters flocked to the exits.

~ 36 ~
Washington Square Park, New York City

Morgan Prince sat on a bench in Washington Square Park in the late afternoon of an early November day. It was a sunny afternoon, about fifty three degrees out, warm enough to bring people outside to enjoy the day. Prince watched as a jogger approached.

Prince stared, recognizing the jogger. He stood from the bench and waved to catch the jogger's attention.

"Steve?" he called.

Steve stopped and stared at him.

"Mr. Prince?" said Steve. "Hi. I'm surprised to see you again. What are you doing here?"

"Hi, Steve. I'm meeting with my younger daughter in a bit," said Morgan. "I always enjoy coming here if I have time."

Steve nodded. "It's a nice park."

"How are things going?" Prince asked. "How's school?"

"It's weird," said Steve. "My life is so different now. Before, I was independent, living on my own, trying to make it," he said. "Now, I'm a student. I'm living in a dorm. I have a roommate. It's weird." He shrugged. "But, so far, it's been a blast."

"I'm happy for you, Steve. You deserve good fortune."

"Thanks, Mr. Prince," said Steve. "I'm amazed that I was given such a phenomenal opportunity."

"Enjoy it. Make the most of it," said Prince. "How did your assignment go, in Baltimore?" he asked.

"Good," said Steve. "The job was simple enough. I just had to drive the client from the hospital to the Maryland House, and then I went back to the city. The worst part of the whole job," he said, "was going back and forth to New York."

"Yes, sometimes travel can be lengthy," said Prince. "You didn't drive the woman back to New York with you?"

"No," said Steve. "I left her with Mr. Bromwell at the Maryland House."

"Ah, I see," said Prince. "Well, congratulations on a successful first job," he said. "Have you posted for any new jobs since?"

"No," said Steve. "I have exams coming up so I need time to study. That's something that I like about the job. It's flexible. I can post for positions when I'm able."

"So, campus life is agreeing with you?" said Prince.

"Yes," said Steve. "It is." He smiled. Steve glanced over Prince's shoulder. "Here comes my roommate. I'll introduce you," he said.

"Jamal!" Steve waved his arms to catch his roommate's attention.

Prince turned as Jamal approached.

Jamal stopped. He removed his ear buds.

"Hi, Steve," said Jamal. "What's up?"

"Hi, Jamal. This is Mr. Prince," said Steve. "Mr. Prince, this is my roommate at NYU. Jamal."

"We've met," said Prince. "Hi, Jamal."

"Hi, Mr. Prince," said Jamal.

"You two know each other?" said Steve.

"Mr. Prince, are you here because of Alicia?"

"Yes, I'm meeting her soon at the coffeehouse."

"You haven't heard?" said Jamal. "Alicia's in the hospital. She was pushed off a subway platform at Times Square this afternoon. I rode in the ambulance with her. I just came from the hospital."

"Alicia was pushed off a subway platform?" said Prince. "Jamal, is she okay?"

"Yes. Samantha saved her," said Jamal.

"Samantha saved her?" said Prince.

"Yes," said Jamal. "Samantha jumped down onto the tracks to help her. When I arrived, Alicia had already been lifted onto the platform. Samantha was still standing on the tracks. I recognized her and asked her if she needed help," said Jamal.

"She asked me to help the girl, so I did," said Jamal. "I realized that it was Alicia. I let Gwen know. "

"Thank you for watching out for her, Jamal," said Prince.

"You're welcome."

Prince's phone chimed. He glanced down at the screen.

"It's Alicia's mother," he said. "Excuse me." He stepped away to take the call.

"Steve, how do you know Mr. Prince?" asked Jamal.

"We met in New Orleans," said Steve. "He prevented me from being mugged on my way to work one night. We discovered that we have a connection in common here in New York."

"Who?"

"My ex-girlfrriend."

"Small world," said Jamal.

"Very small world," said Steve.

"Not only that," said Steve. "But Mr. Prince and I both work for the same company. How's that for coincidence?"

"The security job?" said Jamal.

"Yes," said Steve. "Mr. Prince works for the same company that got me back to New York and into NYU."

"Hmm," said Jamal. "That's pretty amazing."

"Jamal, how do you know Mr. Prince?" asked Steve.

"I met him on a flight to Florida when I was in high school," said Jamal. "Last month, I learned that he's Gwen's birth father."

"Mr. Prince is Gwen's father?" said Steve.

"Yes," said Jamal. "How's that for coincidence?"

~ 37 ~

Mount Sinai Hospital, New York City

Prince found Alicia propped up on pillows in a hospital bed in Mount Sinai. Her left leg was elevated. Her wrist and foot were wrapped in compression bandages. She had ice bags on her knees. She flipped channels on the television remote.

"Hi, Alicia," said Morgan. "Is it okay if I visit?"

"Hi, Morgan." Alicia smiled. "Yes, thank you." She muted the sound on the television. "I'm sorry I couldn't make our meeting. Did Mom tell you I was here?"

"Yes, she did," said Prince, "but, before that, I ran into Jamal in the park. He also told me you were here. How are you?"

"I'm okay," said Alicia. "I'm sore, but I'm okay. I've had sprains before." She shrugged.

"I'm glad that you're okay," said Prince. "You must have been terrified."

"I was terrified," said Alicia. "I didn't know what to do. The train conductor blasted a warning and everybody on the platform was screaming." Alicia shook her head. "So, I got up and took a step toward the platform," she said.

"A woman jumped down on top of me and pushed me into the drainage ditch. The train rolled over both of us. She saved my life," said Alicia. "Jamal knew her. She told me that her name was Samantha."

"Yes," said Prince. "Jamal told me that Samantha was the one who jumped down to help you. I also know her."

"How do you know her?" asked Alicia.

"Jamal, Samantha, and I met on a plane some time ago," said Prince. "I'm glad that Samantha was there to help you to-day."

"Me, too," said Alicia. "Jamal said that Samantha asked him to help me, so he rode in the ambulance with me to the hospital. On the way, he showed me the pictures that he had taken during the day. He said a man yelled at him for taking his photograph."

Alicia smiled. "I like Jamal," she said. "But don't tell Gwen I said that."

"Your secret's safe with me," said Morgan. "But I agree with you. Jamal is a good man."

Prince stopped in the lounge on the main floor of the hospital.

He typed a message on his phone.

'Are you in NYC?'

Samantha's response came quickly.

'Yes. Where are you?'

"I'm also here in the city. Can we meet?"

~ 38 ~
Midtown, New York City

Morgan stood to greet Samantha as she entered the lounge of the midtown hotel.

"Hi, Morgan," said Samantha. "It's amazing that we're both here in the city at the same time."

"It certainly is," said Prince. ""Shall we sit? I took the liberty of ordering tea."

"That sounds excellent," said Samantha.

Samantha and Morgan sat in wing chairs in a corner of the lounge. A server approached with a tray and poured tea.

"Are you here for work?" Samantha asked.

"No. I finished a job earlier, in Paterson," said Morgan. "I came into the city for a visit with my younger daughter."

"Why did you think I might be here?" asked Samantha.

"I ran into Jamal in the park earlier. He told me what happened today," said Prince. "He said you jumped off a subway platform to save a girl."

Samantha shook her head. "Once again, there was Jamal," she said. "I asked him to help the girl."

"He did," said Prince. "He rode in the ambulance with her. Samantha, you saved my daughter today."

"Your daughter?"

"Yes. Alicia. The girl with the violin and the plaid uniform. My daughter," said Prince. "Thank you."

"Alicia," Samantha repeated. "She told me that was her name. I had no idea that she was your daughter. How strange. How is she?"

"She has bruises, scrapes, and sprains," said Morgan, "but she's tough. The hospital is keeping her overnight, just to make sure. I just came from a visit with her."

"I should have stopped the woman from hitting her, in the first place. But the platform was too crowded. I couldn't get there in time."

"Samantha, you saved her."

"I'm glad that I was there to help her," said Samantha.

"Were you working?" asked Prince.

"Yes. I finished a job in Newark and was immediately reassigned to the Times Square subway station. I wasn't given any details about the job."

Samantha shook her head. "How odd that it was your daughter. And that Jamal was there. How does that happen?" she said, shaking her head. "Hmm. Well, now, I've met both of your daughters. Did Jamal know it was Alicia?" she asked.

"Yes. Gwen introduced them on the same night that she introduced Jamal to me," said Prince,

"Ascenda assigned me to protect your daughter," said Samantha. "What does that mean?"

"I don't know," said Prince. "I'm just thankful that she's alive. I'm grateful that the firm sent you to help her. I'm thankful that the firm understands how important my daughters are to me."

"How could the firm know what was going to happen?" Samantha asked.

"I'm not sure," said Prince. "Mr. Bromwell told me that

Ascenda is a top-notch, cutting edge, firm with access to sophisticated technology. Maybe the firm didn't know that Alicia would be the victim," he said. "Maybe the firm somehow knew that the lady with the sword would be on that platform. Maybe the firm didn't know who the victim would be."

"So, you're saying that the firm's technology can identify trouble, like the lady with the sword," said Samantha, "but that her choice of victim was random?"

"Maybe," said Prince. "You were there to help whoever needed it. Today, it was my daughter Alicia."

"Hmm," said Samantha, shaking her head. "And Jamal just happened to be there?"

Prince shrugged. "Maybe. But I learned something else tonight that's a little strange."

"What?" asked Samantha.

"I ran into Steve, my former client from New Orleans, in the park. Steve introduced me to his roommate at NYU," said Prince. "He introduced me to Jamal."

"They're roommates?" said Samantha.

"Yes," said Prince.

"So, let's see," said Samantha. "Steve was your client in New Orleans, assigned to you by the firm. You learned that he saved Ellen from her attempted suicide. Now, he works for Ascenda and is roommates with Jamal."

Samantha shook her head. "We're all connected."

"It seems so," said Prince.

Samantha shook her head.

"So, it's beyond coincidence," she said. "It's Ascenda."

~ 39 ~

New Brunswick, New Jersey

Ceci prepped for happy hour in McGill's Tavern in downtown New Brunswick, New Jersey. She wiped her hands on a bar towel and went to serve her first customer of the night, a businessman dressed in a navy suit and a bright pink tie.

"Hi. What can I get you?"

"I'll have a club soda with lime," said Mr. Bromwell.

Ceci filled a glass with ice and club soda. She twisted a lime onto the glass and placed it on the bar.

"Thank you," said Mr. Bromwell. "Not too busy right now?" he asked.

"No. Soon, we'll get a crowd for happy hour, though."

"Can we have a conversation?"

"Sure," said Ceci.

"Hi. I'm David Bromwell."

"I'm Ceci Torres."

"Have you worked here very long, Ceci?"

"Not in this place," said Ceci. "I've tended bar in a lot of places but I've only been here a few months."

"Is tending bar your future?" Mr. Bromwell asked.

"Right now, it is," said Ceci. "It pays the bills," she said.

"I'm glad to have the job."

"That's an excellent attitude," said Mr. Bromwell. "Are you from New Brunswick?"

"No. I lived in north Jersey before I moved her. I'm auditing a class at Rutgers," said Ceci. "I'd like to apply in the future."

"Hmm," said Mr. Bromwell. "Would you consider a work/study opportunity?"

"Excuse me?" said Ceci.

"Would you be interested in an opportunity that will both pay the bills and help you go to college?"

"Well, sure," said Ceci. "Wouldn't we all?"

Mr. Bromwell handed Ceci his business card.

"What does AS stand for?" asked Ceci.

"Ascenda Security. My firm is always hiring new agents," said Mr. Bromwell. "Perhaps you would be interested."

Ceci stared at him warily. "Why do you say that?"

"I perceive that you're searching for your purpose in life," said Mr. Bromwell. "What if my position were the answer to your search?"

A group of six arrived for happy hour.

"Happy hour begins," said Ceci.

"Well, I won't take up any more of your time," said Mr. Bromwell. He stood up from the bar.

"It was a pleasure meeting you, Ms. Torres. Please keep my card. If you're interested in exploring a position with my firm, please call the number on the back of my card," he said. "Thank you for the conversation."

~ 40 ~

Charlotte, North Carolina

It was the holiday season. Samantha called her mother.

"Happy Birthday, Mom."

"Thank you, Samantha," said Peggy. "Thank you for the lovely birthday gift. I'm wearing the bracelet to dinner tonight."

"What are your plans?"

"Daniel and his boyfriend are cooking dinner for me. Daniel made a cake," said Peggy.

"Do I know Daniel, Mom?" asked Samantha.

"He's Joey's boy."

"Cousin Joey?" said Samantha. "From Alabama?"

"Yes. Daniel is going to school at UC Santa Barbara. He stops in every now and again. I think he's nervous because he's bringing his boyfriend tonight."

"Is Daniel a good cook?" Samantha asked.

"Oh, yes," said Peggy.

"Well, it sounds fun. Enjoy."

"Thank you, honey," said Peggy. "Are you at home?"

"Yes, I arrived home from Atlanta last night and I'm leaving tomorrow for a weeklong job in New York City."

"No time off between jobs?" said Peggy.

"No," said Samantha. "The holidays are a busy time at work."

"Do you think that you can find some time to come out here to visit?" Peggy asked.

"I might be able to get out there for New Year's, Mom," said Samantha. "Would that work for you?"

"I'd love that," said Peggy. "It would be so much fun. I could introduce you to Harold."

"Sure, Mom," said Samantha. "How are you doing?"

"I still miss my Stanley," said Peggy, "but I'm finding pleasure in new things. How are you doing?"

"I still miss Kip," she said, "but, like you, I'm finding pleasure in new things. I've developed a friendship with my downstairs neighbor and her children."

"That's good to hear, Samantha," said Peggy.

"Mom, I've been thinking about inviting Kip's family for Christmas tea. What do you think?"

"It sounds like a wonderful idea."

"Okay, good. I'm going to do it," said Samantha. "Happy Birthday, Mom. Enjoy your dinner with Daniel and his boyfriend. I'll confirm my visit once I get clearance," she said.

"Oh, Samantha, I can't wait," said Peggy.

Samantha reread her invitation to Kip's family.

'Merry Christmas! Are you available for afternoon tea on Sunday, the 20th?'

Lynn Fields replied quickly.

'Happy Holidays, Samantha. We'd love to join you. We all look forward to seeing you.'

Samantha hung the last ornament on her Christmas tree.

"One more," said Rosa. "From us."

Samantha unwrapped the small package to reveal a sleek crystal bird ornament.

"I love it! It's perfect," said Samantha. "Thank you."

The children smiled.

"Where will you put it?" asked Carla.

"I think this is a good spot," said Samantha. She hung the ornament below a string of white lights.

"Okay, Johnny, plug it in."

The crystal bird reflected the white lights from the string above it.

The children clapped.

Samantha brought out two wrapped presents from her hall closet. She handed the boxes to the children.

"You can't open them until Christmas Day. No shaking and no peeking. Do you think you can do that?"

"I can do it," said Johnny, nodding, hugging the box.

"I think I can do it," said Carla.

Samantha smiled.

~ 41 ~

Herald Square, New York City

Holiday visitors crowded the pedestrian zone in Herald Square. Morgan Prince reread the message on his wrist device.

'Camouflage sneakers'.

Prince spotted a young man wearing sneakers matching that description.

The man tied his shoes against a planter near the end of the pedestrian zone. He tossed something into the planter, then glanced around at the people nearest him. He stepped through the opening in the large boulders that marked the end of the pedestrian zone. The man crossed the street.

Prince found the paper bag inside the planter. He alerted a nearby police officer. He left the park in pursuit of the man who had placed the bag in the planter.

Prince entered the Herald Square subway station.

He checked each platform.

He saw no sign of the man in the camouflage sneakers.

~ 42 ~

Astor Coffeehouse, New York City

Jamal and Gwen met in the Astor Coffeehouse on the night of the annual holiday tree lighting in Washington Square Park.

"Hi, Gwen," said Jamal. He rubbed his hands together. "If we're going to be outside, I need to go back and get my gloves."

"You're such a baby," said Gwen.

"It's cold."

"Jamal, are you backing out?" said Gwen.

"No. I just need a pair of gloves," said Jamal.

Gwen pulled an extra pair from her backpack.

"Try these."

Jamal pulled the gloves on. He nodded. "Okay. Thanks."

"Is Steve meeting us here?" Gwen asked.

"No. He can't make it," said Jamal. "He got called in for a last-minute job tonight."

"Tending bar?" said Gwen.

"No. His other job," said Jamal. "I think he had to drive a car to Philadelphia, or something like that."

"Okay. Too bad," said Gwen. She held up a gift card. "Coffee's on me. It's an early Christmas present from my mom."

~ 43 ~

Washington Square Park, New York City

It was the fourth day of Samantha's assignment in New York City. On the first day, she had been assigned to stop the mugging of an elderly man in Times Square. On her second day, she had helped a runaway in the Port Authority Bus Station. On her third day, she had helped with a medical emergency on 27th Street. She visited the park on the night of the annual tree lighting while she waited for her next assignment.

Police officers patrolled the grounds. Park employees in bright orange jackets flanked the holiday tree near the Arch. A few carolers started to sing. The crowd around the tree grew.

Samantha stepped away.

She sat on a park bench and watched the people streaming by her on their way to the event.

A man wearing the bright orange jacket of the park employees stood near the front hedge. The man wore a hoodie underneath his orange jacket, with the hood pulled up over his head. He knelt to tie the laces of his camouflage sneakers. He stood and quickly made his way to the exit.

Samantha found a small black metal box under the front hedge. She alerted a police officer.

She read the officer's badge.

"Officer Nathan," she said. "You need to evacuate the park. There could be other bombs. I'm going after him. I'll contact you when I come back. My name is Samantha."

Samantha exited the park. She caught a flash of orange across the intersection. Car horns blared as she crossed against the light.

Samantha hurried forward, searching for the man wearing the orange jacket. She spied a flash of orange on the next block.

An elderly man sat against a storefront, the orange jacket draped over him.

"Which way did he go, sir?" Samantha asked.

The man pointed down the block.

Samantha weaved through the surrounding streets, searching for the man in the camouflage sneakers.

A police officer stood in front of the crowd gathered at the holiday tree near the Arch. He waved his hands to quiet the carolers.

"Folks," he said, "the tree lighting has been canceled for tonight. I ask for your cooperation in leaving the park immediately."

The crowd booed.

"It's supposed to be tonight!" a woman yelled.

"I'm sorry for the inconvenience," said the officer.

"Why is it canceled?" a woman called out.

"Police investigation," said the officer.

"Listen, folks," he said, "to ensure public safety, we need everyone to leave the park. Officers, in uniform, and park employees, in orange jackets, will help to safely usher everyone to the exits. Thank you for your cooperation."

Samantha gave up her search for the man who had left the black metal box. She returned to the park. She stepped up to the tow officers who flanked the park entrance.

"Park's closed!" said one of the officers.

"Officers," said Samantha. "I was the one who found the bomb. I pursued the suspect but lost him. Would you please contact Officer Nathan?"

Officers with bomb-sniffing dogs patrolled the grounds as Samantha gained entry to the park. Police officers stood in clusters on the lawn. The bomb squad had arrived.

Samantha stood on the lawn near the oak tree. She watched as the bomb squad deployed a robot to defuse the bomb left under the front hedge.

Jamal and Gwen moved along the queue of people exiting the park at the Arch. Jamal noticed the cluster of police uniforms standing on the lawn near the oak tree. He recognized Samantha standing near them.

"Samantha's here," said Jamal. "Over there on the lawn. I need to see if she needs help." He stepped out of the line.

"Please step back in line, sir," said two officers who approached. "Let's go, folks."

"Officers, I know that woman over there," said Jamal. "I have to help her."

"We've got it covered, sir. Let's go."

The officers escorted Jamal and Gwen out of the park.

"Gwen I have to get back inside," said Jamal. "I'll find you later." He walked away to find a way in to the park.

Gwen followed behind him.

Patrol cars were haphazardly parked on the street at the next entrance. A cluster of officers stood on the sidewalk outside the entrance.

Jamal approached the next entrance.

A police officer stood alone at the entrance, struggling to keep people from entering. Jamal pushed his way through the crowd.

"Park's closed, park's closed!" the officer yelled. "The event is canceled for tonight!"

Jamal stepped alongside the officer at the entrance. He faced the crowd of people trying to gain entry.

"Park's closed! Park's closed!" Jamal yelled.

"Who are you?" said the officer.

Jamal slipped through the entrance.

Gwen stepped up behind him.

The officer shook his head.

"Park's closed!" he yelled.

Morgan Prince arrived at Washington Square Park. His wrist device buzzed.

'*Camouflage sneakers in park.*'

Police officers blocked Prince at the park entrance.

"Park's closed! The tree lighting has been canceled for tonight!" an officer yelled.

"Officers, I believe that it's the same guy who just left a bomb in Herald Square. I can help to identify him."

"We've got it covered, sir. Please step back."

Prince stepped away from the entrance.

"Morgan?"

"Gwen? Hi," said Prince. "It's nice to run into you, Gwen, but I can't chat right now. I'm working. I have to get inside the park."

"That's what Jamal said."

"Jamal's here?" said Prince.

"Yes. The police evacuated us from the park but Jamal

got back inside," said Gwen. "I tried but I couldn't get in. Jamal went to help Samantha, the woman we met in Baltimore. She was standing near the oak tree."

"Samantha's here, too?" said Morgan.

"Yes."

"I've got to help them," said Morgan.

"I'll come with you," said Gwen.

"Gwen, no," said Morgan. "I need you to be safe. I'll find you later."

"That's what Jamal said." Gwen shook her head.

Officers ushered the remaining stragglers out of the park near the Arch as Prince climbed over a railing and pushed through the hedge to enter the park.

~ 44 ~

Washington Square Park, New York City

Samantha saw the man in the SWAT team vest standing near her on the park lawn. The man wore camouflage sneakers and a black hoodie under his vest. He swiped the screen on his phone.

Samantha moved behind him. She rushed forward, knocking the man down onto the ground. She called out to the nearby police officers.

"Help!" she yelled. "He's the bomber!"

Police officers approached as the man got to his feet.

"Officers, this lady assaulted me!" he said. "I was minding my own business when she attacked me!"

"He's the bomber!" yelled Samantha. She charged at the man again, knocking the back of his head against the trunk of the tree. The man bounced off the tree and fell forward onto the ground. His phone flew up out of his hands.

An officer bent to pick it up.

"That's okay. I don't need the phone," the man said. He got up from the ground. He touched the back of his head and winced. He leaned back against the tree.

Police officers circled Samantha and the man.

"I surrender." The man held up his hands, defensively.

Jamal reached the circle of officers. He struggled with police officers who held him back.

"Samantha!" he called out. "Samantha, how can I help you?"

"Jamal, just stay back," said Samantha.

Jamal tried to break free of the officers' grip.

"No, Jamal! Stay back!" yelled Samantha.

Morgan Prince reached the circle of officers. He saw Jamal struggling with the officers. He saw Samantha standing inside the circle with the man in the camouflage sneakers.

Prince pushed through the circle of officers.

"Let her go!" Prince called to the man.

"No. I don't think so."

"Let her go. You can have me instead," said Prince.

"No, Morgan!" said Samantha.

"No," said the man. "I'm afraid not. You're welcome to join us, though."

"Morgan, no!" said Samantha.

"Sir, can we talk a bit?" said Prince.

"I think I'll just let this wire do my talking."

The man showed a wire that ran across his palm and disappeared up his arm.

"No!" Jamal charged forward.

Prince followed him.

"Here's to eternity."

The man in the SWAT vest pulled the wire. A bomb exploded in his backpack.

Prince took cover.

Jamal ran forward until the shrapnel cut him down.

Prince stood after the explosion. He glanced at the oak tree and quickly looked away. Jamal lay on the ground. Shrapnel had pierced his face and neck. It had sliced through his jacket. Shrapnel had shredded his gloves.

Prince knelt down next to Jamal. He placed two fingers on Jamal's wrist.

"Jamal, can you hear me?" Prince called.

Jamal's eyelids fluttered open.

"Mr. Prince," Jamal murmured. "Tell my grandmother." His eyes closed again.

"I'll call her, Jamal. I'll tell her you're going to be fine. Let me just get your phone." He found Jamal's cell phone in the pocket of his jacket.

"Jamal, I'll have Gwen return your phone to you tomorrow. Everything's going to be okay."

Jamal's eyes fluttered but didn't open.

"Jamal, you're going to be fine, Jamal," said Prince.

Sirens announced the arrival of ambulances.

The EMTs loaded Jamal into the back of an ambulance along with several injured police officers.

"Jamal, you're in good hands," said Prince. "I have to find Gwen. I'll stop by to see you later."

~ 45 ~
New York City

Prince found Gwen standing behind a police barricade across the street from the park entrance.

"Gwen, are you okay?" Prince asked.

"Yes. Are you? There was a bomb?"

"Yes," said Morgan.

"Where's Jamal?"

"He was injured in the blast," said Prince. "An ambulance took him to the hospital."

"Is he okay?" asked Gwen.

"He took a lot of shrapnel," said Morgan. "He'll need time but I think he'll be okay. Jamal ran into the explosion."

"To help Samantha?" said Gwen.

"Yes," said Morgan. "A guy near Samantha in a SWAT vest showed a wire in his hand and Jamal started running. He was fiercely brave."

"Is Samantha okay?" Gwen asked.

Morgan shook his head. "She was killed in the explosion. Jamal and several officers were injured."

Gwen frowned. "Does Jamal know?"

"I think so," said Prince. "I'm not sure."

"Where did the ambulance take him?"

"Mount Sinai," said Morgan. "I told him that I'd check in on him after I found you. Would you like to walk with me?"

Morgan and Gwen waited for the street light to change.

"I dragged Jamal to the park tonight for the tree lighting," said Gwen. "I wish we hadn't gone." She frowned.

"Gwen, the circumstances tonight were well out of your control," said Prince.

"You said you were working," said Gwen. "Was Samantha?"

"I don't know," said Morgan. "It's possible. It's also possible that she just noticed something off about the guy and discovered the bomb, then acted to save lives."

Gwen frowned. "I can't believe that she's gone. Jamal will be very upset."

"Jamal did everything he could," said Prince. "I wish that I had done more."

"What do you mean?"

"The same guy planted a bomb earlier in Herald Square," said Morgan. "I prevented a bombing there but I let the bomber escape. If I had stopped him at Herald Square, none of this would have happened."

Morgan and Gwen took seats in the waiting room in Mount Sinai Hospital.

Prince called Jamal's grandmother. He explained that he and Gwen were in the waiting room of Mount Sinai while Jamal was in surgery to remove shrapnel from his body after the explosion in the park.

Prince offered to call Jamal's grandmother when Jamal came out of surgery.

Gwen looked up from her phone.

"My mother has invited you to join us for breakfast tomorrow morning. What should I tell her?"

"Tell her I accept."

"Are you sure?" said Gwen. "It will be me, Alicia, my Mom, and my Dad."

"Tell your mother that I accept," said Morgan.

"Okay," said Gwen, shaking her head. "Worlds collide."

"Morgan, did you know that I met Samantha with Jamal in Baltimore?"

"Yes. I ran into Samantha on the day after you met her," said Morgan. "She was very surprised to discover that you were my daughter and that you and Jamal were friends."

"Were you and Samantha in regular contact?"

"No. Our schedules make it hard to maintain any kind of regular contact," said Morgan. "But, we ran into each other, from time to time."

"Why are you, Jamal, and Samantha so connected?" Gwen asked.

"Well, I learned that Samantha was also a near-death survivor," said Morgan. "I think that shared experience created a bond between us."

Gwen squinted at him.

"I remember when you came home from the hospital after your heart attack," she said. "You told us that you saw heaven. Mom got mad when you talked about it."

"It was such a phenomenal experience that I droned on to anybody who would listen," said Morgan. "I think that I embarrassed your mother."

"I could see that," said Gwen, nodding.

"Okay, so, that's why you and Samantha were connected," she said. "Why was Jamal so connected to her?"

"I guess they developed their own bond," said Morgan.

Gwen frowned.

The phone rang on the empty desk in the waiting room.

Morgan picked up the receiver.

A nurse told him that Jamal was out of surgery and was being moved to the recovery room.

~ 46 ~

Broome Street Diner, New York City

Alicia met Morgan at the entrance to the Broome Street Diner in Greenwich Village. She led him to the family's booth.

"Good morning," said Morgan. He took the empty seat next to Marie's husband Dan. Marie sat across from him, flanked by the girls.

"Good morning, Morgan," said Marie. "Thanks for joining us. I know it's been a trying time. Please know that we're here to help in any way that we can."

"Thank you," said Morgan.

Morgan pulled Jamal's phone from his pocket.

"Gwen, I told Jamal that I'd have you get this back to him this morning. Is that okay? I probably won't get to the hospital until later tonight. I'm sure his grandmother would like to talk to him before then, if he's able."

"Sure," said Gwen. "I'll drop it off on my break between my morning classes." She zipped it into her backpack.

The server arrived at the table to take their order.

"Morgan, Gwen's told us about the explosion last night," said Marie. "What else can you tell us?"

"I prevented a bombing last night in Herald Square,"

said Prince. "The bomber escaped in Herald Square. He tried again in Washington Square Park," he said. "The bomb squad successfully defused the bomb he left under a hedge," he said.

"I don't know why Samantha was in the park," said Prince, "but she was standing near the bomber when he detonated a bomb in his backpack. Samantha was killed, and Jamal and several officers were injured."

"Gwen said that you and Jamal both knew Samantha," said Marie.

"Yes. The three of us met on a flight to Florida."

"Morgan, is she the same lady who helped me in the subway?" Alicia asked.

"Yes," said Morgan.

Alicia frowned.

"She was?" said Marie. "Alicia told us that you knew the woman who helped her in the subway. I'm forever grateful to her for saving Alicia. I didn't realize that she was the same woman. What a terrible tragedy," said Marie. She frowned, shaking her head.

"Morgan, how does Gwen fit into this?" she asked.

"Mom, I don't fit into it, " said Gwen. "Morgan had nothing to do with me being at the park last night. I told you that Jamal and I are friends. We went to the park for the tree lighting. And, Jamal was the one who introduced me to Samantha, not Morgan."

"We're just trying to understand it, honey," said Dan.

Gwen sighed. "The tree lighting was canceled," she said. "The police evacuated the park. Jamal and I left but he saw Samantha standing on the lawn and he went back inside to help her. That's what happened."

"Honey, it's just concerning to have you involved in any way with this," said Marie. She glanced at Morgan.

Gwen frowned.

Marie held Morgan back outside the restaurant as the girls walked up the sidewalk with Dan.

"Morgan, are the girls safe?" asked Marie."I'm concerned that they're somehow connected to this. Whatever this is," she said. "It's a little unnerving to realize how close Gwen was to danger last night."

"Marie, I have no reason to believe that the girls are in any danger," said Prince. "Gwen was in the park with Jamal for the tree lighting, like a lot of other people."

"Gwen needs to focus on her studies," said Marie. "She can't get involved in dangerous schemes," she said.

"The girls seem comfortable with their contact with you," said Marie. "I won't stop it. I just hope that letting you back in wasn't a mistake."

~ 47 ~
Mount Sinai Hospital, New York City

Gwen entered Jamal's hospital room during her break between morning classes. Jamal was asleep.

A nurse breezed into the room.

"He's been sleeping all morning," the nurse said. "He missed breakfast."

"Is he okay?" asked Gwen.

"Well, he's banged up pretty badly," said the nurse, "but we're watching him closely," she said. "Don't worry. We're taking good care of him." The nurse nodded.

"Okay. Thanks. I'm just leaving his phone for him."

"Oh, sure," said the nurse. "You can put it in the drawer in the tray. If he wakes during my shift, I'll tell him it's there. If not, I'll let the new shift nurse know."

"Okay. Thank you," said Gwen. She wrote a note to Jamal and left it on top of his tray.

Gwen returned to the hospital after her classes ended for the day. Jamal was awake when she stepped into the room.

"Hi, Jamal," said Gwen. "I'm glad to see that you're

awake. Are you okay to have a visitor?"

"Yes. Hi, Gwen. Come in," said Jamal. "Thanks for visiting. And for dropping my phone off this morning."

Gwen eyed Jamal's bandaged body.

"How are you feeling?" she asked.

"Okay. Mostly sore. My whole body stings."

"Morgan said that you ran into the explosion."

"I just wanted to help her," said Jamal.

"Morgan said that you were fiercely brave."

"I couldn't help her," said Jamal, shrugging.

"Morgan said that you did everything that you could, Jamal," said Gwen.

"It wasn't enough," said Jamal.

"I'm sorry, Jamal. I know that she was important to you."

Jamal nodded.

"She was important to Morgan, too," said Gwen. "Last night, while we were in the waiting room, Morgan told me that his connection to Samantha was because they were both near-death survivors. He said that he discovered it on the flight to Florida."

"They talked about it on the plane," said Jamal. "Samantha asked me if I was one," he said. "She asked me if I could make it 'three for three.'"

"Three for three?"

"Three near-death survivors seated in the same row of an airplane," said Jamal.

"Are you a near-death survivor, too?" Gwen asked.

"I didn't realize it at the time," said Jamal, "but I thought about it when I got home. I survived two near fatal incidents when I was young."

"So, that's why you were so connected to Samantha?"

"That, and the fact that Samantha saved my life," said Jamal. "I'm forever grateful to her. I just wish I could have returned the favor."

"Jamal, how did Samantha save your life?"

"She came into the store where I worked one New Year's Eve and warned me to stay home that night. She paid for a loaf of bread with three dollar bills. Each of the bills was defaced with a message written in marker pens. 'Stay home. Don't get into a car tonight. Live to see the new year.' I still have those bills."

"That's weird, Jamal," said Gwen.

"Maybe, but it worked," said Jamal. "Having Samantha deliver the message made me take it seriously. My friends died that night. I stayed home and lived. I credit Samantha for saving my life."

"How could she have known?"

"She said that she didn't know. She said that she was on a training task for her new job. Her task was to persuade the clerk on Lane #8 to stay home. She said that she didn't know that I'd be the clerk," said Jamal.

"Who hired her firm to persuade you?"

"She didn't know. She only followed the instructions for the task," said Jamal. "That night, I told her that I was like her and Mr. Prince."

"So, all three of you are near-death survivors," said Gwen, "and she saved your life?"

Jamal nodded.

"That's really weird, Jamal," said Gwen.

"Hmm," she said. "I once canceled plans to go out on New Year's Eve at the last minute. My friends died in a car crash on the way home. I stayed home and lived. That's weird that we have that in common."

"Why did you cancel your plans?" Jamal asked.

"I had a missed call from Morgan," said Gwen. "At the time, we hadn't been in contact for a few years so it was unusual for him to call. He didn't leave a message or a text. I waited for him to call me back but he never did."

"But his missed call made you stay home?"

"Yes," said Gwen. "I guess I can credit him with saving my life that night."

"Does Morgan know?" said Jamal.

"Neither one of us has mentioned it," said Gwen. "Sometimes, I wonder if it was just a technology glitch."

"What kind of glitch?" asked Jamal.

"Maybe my number was mistakenly dialed from Morgan's phone," said Gwen. "Or the call was spoofed to look like Morgan's phone, thinking I'd pick up."

"You've thought about this," said Jamal.

"We had been out of touch for a while so his call was really unexpected," said Gwen.

"Why didn't you just return the call?" asked Jamal.

"I just wasn't comfortable calling him," she said.

Gwen shook her head.

"You know, last night was the most time that Morgan and I have spent in years."

"How was it?" asked Jamal.

"It was okay," said Gwen.

~ 48 ~

Mount Sinai Hospital, New York City

Steve knocked on the door of Jamal's hospital room.

"Hey, Jamal," said Steve. "Are you up for a visit?"

"Hi, Steve. Sure, come in," said Jamal. "Thanks for stopping. How did your job go last night?"

"It was pretty simple," said Steve. "I drove a car to Philly and took the train back. You weren't there when I got in but I figured you'd show up at some point. I was tired and fell asleep. It wasn't until this morning when I got a text from Gwen that I learned what happened. How are you feeling?"

"I'm sore but they tell me that I'll be okay."

"Gwen said that a guy detonated a bomb in the park. She said that it killed a woman that you know?"

"Yes. Samantha," said Jamal. He frowned.

"I'm sorry, Jamal," said Steve. "How do you know her?"

"Mr. Prince, Samantha, and I were seat mates on a flight to Florida. I've been running into her on occasion."

"Why was she in the park?" asked Steve.

"I'm not sure," said Jamal. "I didn't get a chance to talk to her. The police evacuated the park. I saw her standing inside and went back to help her but I was too late."

"I'm sorry, Jamal," said Steve.

"Thanks," said Jamal.

"If I hadn't gotten that last minute assignment, I would have been with you and Gwen in the park," said Steve. "Maybe, if we were both there, we could have stopped the guy."

"I don't know," said Jamal. "Mr. Prince was there but he wasn't able to help, either. It happened so fast. The guy showed a wire in his hand and detonated a bomb in his backpack. Samantha was killed in the blast." Jamal shook his head. "Maybe it was good that you weren't there," he said. "You could be lying here like me. Your job kept you out of danger last night."

Steve nodded. "I guess it did."

"Hmm. Can I ask you something?" said Jamal.

"What's that?" said Steve.

"You told me that the man who offered you the job with Ascenda knew that you saved your ex-girlfriend."

"Yes," said Steve.

"You said he also knew that a fire killed your parents," said Jamal. "What happened?"

"I got home and found that the house was on fire," said Steve. "I went inside to try to save my parents but I blacked out from smoke inhalation. The firefighters found me. I survived but my parents didn't."

"Do you remember anything from when you blacked out?" asked Jamal.

Steve squinted at Jamal. He shrugged.

"I remember one thing," said Steve. "I guess I dreamed it. It seemed real, though. I saw my grandmother. She shook her finger at me. She said it was too soon. I've always wondered about that," said Steve. "Too soon for what, exactly?" He shrugged.

"I think I might have an idea," said Jamal.

~ 49 ~

Mount Sinai Hospital, New York City

Morgan Prince stepped into Jamal's hospital room.

"Jamal, hi. Is it okay if I visit?"

"Hi. Yes, thank you," said Jamal. "Mr. Prince, thank you for calling my grandmother last night. She said that you helped to calm her down."

Prince smiled. "I'm glad that I was able to lessen your grandmother's worry," he said. "I told her that you would be fine, given time and rest. And you will be."

"That's what they're telling me here," said Jamal..

"How are you feeling?"

Jamal touched the bandages on his face. "I'm sore," he said. "But they say that I'll get better. I'm glad that I'm alive." He frowned. "Samantha's gone, Mr. Prince."

"Yes. I know. I can't stop thinking about it."

"I wish I could have saved her," said Jamal.

"You tried, Jamal. You were so brave."

"I couldn't see a way to stop it," said Jamal. He closed his eyes and shook his head.

"Jamal, you did everything that you could," said Prince.

"I just keep thinking about what I could have done differently," said Jamal. "What if I had gotten into the park sooner? What if I had avoided being evacuated from the park, in the first place? Would that have changed things?"

"I don't know, Jamal," said Prince. "But Samantha knew the danger. She couldn't ask you to help her this time. She wanted you to be safe."

Jamal frowned.

"Do you know if she was working last night?" he asked.

"I don't know," said Prince. "I didn't know she was in the city. It's possible she was working but hard to know for sure."

"I wish I could have saved her," said Jamal.

"I do too, Jamal," said Prince. "I blame myself."

"You? Why?" asked Jamal.

"I was assigned to prevent a bombing in Herald Square earlier in the evening. I was successful in preventing the bomb from detonating but I failed to capture the bomber. I lost him in the subway station. If I had only captured him in Herald Square, Samantha might still be alive."

"Mr. Prince, you and Steve both work for Ascenda. Did Samantha?"

"Yes," said Prince. "She did. When she got back to Charlotte after her house-sitting job in Fort Lauderdale, she was offered a position with the firm."

"I thought that she might," said Jamal. He shook his head.

"Mr. Prince, when I met you and Samantha on the plane, I never expected to see either of you again. But, then, for some reason, Samantha came to Freeport on New Year's Eve and saved my life. Did you know that?"

"Yes. She told me," said Prince. "She was very surprised that you were her client that night."

"We were both surprised," said Jamal. "That night, I told Samantha that I was like you and her. Did she tell you that?"

"Yes," said Prince.

"So, you, Samantha, and I are all near-death survivors," said Jamal.

"It seems so."

"And you, Samantha, and Steve worked for Ascenda. I don't work for the firm but I seem to be connected to it through the three of you."

Prince nodded.

"I think Steve is a near-death survivor, too," said Jamal. "He told me that he survived a fire that killed his parents."

"I didn't know that," said Prince.

"Do you think that it makes us different?" Jamal asked.

"Different? How?" asked Prince.

"Has it changed us?" Jamal asked.

"I don't know, Jamal."

"After Samantha saved me on New Year's Eve," said Jamal, "I kept running into her. I was on a school art trip to Dallas, and there she was. Gwen and I were at the Maryland House, and there she was. I was there when Samantha helped Alicia. And, last night, Gwen and I were in the park. It's strange."

"Samantha also found it strange, Jamal. She joked that, sometimes, if felt like you were her apprentice."

"It felt like that to me, too," said Jamal. "I've been lying here thinking that maybe Ascenda Security is responsible for everything that's happened."

"Jamal, Samantha thought the same thing," said Prince. "What convinced her was that you and Steve are roommates. That was beyond coincidence, she said."

Jamal nodded.

"Mr. Prince, do you think that Ascenda Security is a network of near-death survivors?" asked Jamal. "People who are recruited to help others after getting saved themselves?"

"Jamal, I don't know for sure. I guess it's possible."

"I've been lying here thinking that maybe Ascenda Security is responsible for saving my life in the first place," said Jamal.

"How is that?" Prince squinted at Jamal.

"I'm not entirely clear," said Jamal. "But, strangely, a woman named Lila helped me survive twice when I was young. I've been thinking that maybe Lila is in the network, too."

"Well, it wasn't Lila who brought me back after my heart failure," said Prince. "Alicia's voice brought me back."

Jamal shook his head.

"I haven't figured it all out yet," said Jamal. "I've just been lying here, thinking about it, thinking about everything that's happened since I met you and Samantha on the plane. I've been trying to understand it."

"Jamal, maybe the only thing that matters is that we survived. We've been given another chance at life and we're now trying to help others."

"My grandmother tells me to not to worry about it," said Jamal. "She tells me to just accept the blessing."

"That sounds like good advice, Jamal," said Prince.

Jamal sighed.

"Mr. Prince, is Ascenda Security my future?"

Prince shrugged. "I couldn't say, Jamal."

"And what about Gwen? Is she involved?" Jamal asked. "Or is she just a random connection?"

Prince shook his head. "I don't know, Jamal."

"Mr. Prince, I feel like I'm involved in something I don't understand," said Jamal. "Would it be okay if you and I kept in touch?"

"I'd like that, Jamal."

~ 50 ~

Washington Square Park, New York City

Morgan Prince sat on a bench in Washington Square Park and stared at the scarred oak tree on the park lawn. His gaze tracked to the spot where Jamal had fallen.

A woman sat down on the bench. She wore a long black coat, tall black boots, and a black beret. A small black briefcase rested on her lap. She met Prince's glance.

"Mr. Prince?" she said.

"Excuse me. Do I know you?"

"Mr. Prince, it's me, Ellen." She smiled.

"Ellen? I didn't recognize you. You look very different. Hello. How are you?"

"I'm good," said Ellen. "I have a new job."

"You left the tea shop?"

"Yes," said Ellen. "My manager left so I took advantage of another opportunity."

"Well, congratulations," said Prince. "How is the new job going?"

"So far, so good," said Ellen. "I'm still in training."

"Well, good luck with it," said Prince.

"Thank you," said Ellen. She followed Prince's gaze to

the scarred oak tree.

"You were staring up at that tree when we met," said Ellen.

Prince nodded. "It's such a majestic tree. Unfortunately, it's forever marked by the blast," he said. "And it's a reminder of my friend who died in the explosion."

"I'm very sorry for the loss of your friend, Mr. Prince."

"Thank you, Ellen. That scarred tree is forever a reminder of my failure."

"What failure, Mr. Prince?" said Ellen.

"If I had only captured the bomber in Herald Square, when I had the opportunity to do so, none of this would have happened. My friend would be alive. But I failed to stop him. I failed my friend."

"Mr. Prince, I have a message for you," said Ellen.

"A message?"

"Yes. Your performance was satisfactory on the Herald Square job. You completed the job. You are not to blame for what happened here," said Ellen.

"What?" Prince stared at her.

"You were assigned too late to change the outcome in Washington Square Park," said Ellen. "It's not your fault."

Prince squinted at her. "I don't understand," he said.

"Mr. Prince, things aren't always in our control."

Prince frowned. He shook his head.

Ellen stood from the bench. She placed the strap of her briefcase over her shoulder.

"It was nice seeing you again, Mr. Prince. Perhaps we'll meet again soon." Ellen waved and walked away.

Prince stared as she walked away. He noticed the laminated tag hanging from her briefcase. He stared at the familiar logo on the tag, the two red italic letters set on a glossy black background.

~ 51 ~

Washington Square Park, New York City

Jamal focused his camera on the scarred oak tree in Washington Square Park. He raised his camera to capture a man sitting alone on a park bench in the morning mist.

The man held up his hand. He beckoned to Jamal.

Jamal approached him. "Good morning, sir," he said.

"Good morning."

"I think that we've met before," said Jamal. "In Bryant Park. You asked me not to take your picture."

"Yes, that's right."

"I didn't take any photos this time. I was just about to, when you held up your hand."

"Thank you. I suppose formal introductions are in order. I'm David Bromwell."

"I'm Jamal Williams."

"Can we have a conversation?"

"Excuse me, sir?" said Jamal.

"Are you a college student?"

"Yes. I'm a freshman at NYU."

"Do you have an internship for this coming summer?"

"No," said Jamal. "But I have a summer job at home."

"Perhaps you would be interested in an internship with my firm."

Jamal squinted at him, wary. "Excuse me, sir?"

Mr. Bromwell produced a business card from his pocket and handed it to Jamal.

"I manage a state of the art security operation."

Jamal stared down at the two red letters on the front of the black card. He squinted at Mr. Bromwell.

"Ascenda Security?"

"Yes, that's right. You've heard of the firm?"

"Yes," said Jamal, nodding.

"Are you interested in an internship?"

"Why me, sir?" said Jamal.

Mr. Bromwell glanced at the oak tree. "I understand that you showed fierce courage in your attempt to save a life here," he said.

"How do you know that?" Jamal asked.

"Mr. Williams, I run a top-notch firm. It's my business to know."

Jamal glanced at the tree. "I wasn't able to save her."

"Things aren't always in our control."

Jamal nodded.

"An internship with my firm would expose you to the talent and technology involved in running an operation that is tops in the security industry," said Mr. Bromwell. "It's possible that it could lead to a year-round position, in accordance with your school schedule, of course."

"Like Steve?" said Jamal.

"The internship would specifically be tailored for you."

Jamal fingered the red letters on the card.

"Can I ask you something?" Jamal asked.

"What's on your mind?" said Mr. Bromwell.

"Mr. Bromwell, is Ascenda Security a network of near-death survivors?"

"Jamal, Ascenda Security is a large, global security firm," said Mr. Bromwell. "Our employees demonstrate the talent and commitment to saving lives."

"Is the firm how everyone is connected?" said Jamal.

"The firm prides itself on the connections made among our employees," said Mr. Bromwell.

"Mr. Bromwell, was I Samantha's apprentice?"

"Did you learn from her?" asked Mr. Bromwell.

"Yes," said Jamal.

"Then, it appears that you may have been her apprentice," said Mr. Bromwell.

Jamal shook his head.

"Did the firm arrange my meetings with Samantha? Does the firm use technology to manipulate situations?"

"Coincidences do happen, Jamal."

"It seems like it's more than coincidence," said Jamal.

He squinted at Mr. Bromwell.

"Did Ascenda save me when I was a child?" Jamal asked. "Does Lila work for Ascenda? Am I being called into service? Is Ascenda my future?"

Mr. Bromwell smiled.

"Jamal, I'm offering you an opportunity to explore a summer internship with my security firm," said Mr. Bromwell. "It's been a pleasure meeting you. If you have any interest in the internship, please call the number on the back of my card. My assistant Krista will arrange everything." He stood from the bench.

"Mr. Bromwell, thank you for the opportunity," said Jamal. "I'm just a little overwhelmed at the moment. Can I take some time to think it over?"

"Of course," said Mr. Bromwell. "Take all the time you need, Jamal. Thank you for the conversation."

~ 52 ~

Astor Coffeehouse, New York City

Gwen Prince arrived at the Astor Coffeehouse for an interview for a summer internship. Her Probability Theory professor at NYU had recommended her for the position. Gwen rehearsed answers to interview questions in her head.

A man wearing a dark gray suit and a burgundy tie, with a matching pocket square, approached her table.

"Excuse me. Are you Ms. Prince?"

"Yes. Hello. I'm Gwen Prince."

"Hello. I'm David Bromwell." He gave her his business card. He took a seat at the table.

"You come highly recommended," said Mr. Bromwell.

"Professor Gary is very kind," said Gwen. "He's an excellent teacher. I really enjoy his class."

"What do you like about it?"

"The class helps me to frame the approach to solving problems."

"Can you give me an example?" said Mr. Bromwell.

"Well, lately, I've been trying to calculate the probability of a highly unusual event," said Gwen.

"What would that be?"

"I've been attempting to calculate the probability that three near-death survivors would be seated together in the same row of an airplane," said Gwen.

"That's an interesting problem," said Mr. Bromwell. "Have you arrived at a solution yet?"

"No," said Gwen. "Not yet. I'm still working on it."

"I suppose that a complex problem like that will require significant time to reach a solution."

"Yes," said Gwen, nodding. "Thank you for the opportunity with your firm, Mr. Bromwell. Can you tell me a little bit about the internship? Professor Gary told me that you run a high-technology firm?"

"It's actually a state of the art security firm," said Mr. Bromwell, "but our success is due in large part to the sophisticated technology used in our operation. It's what has kept us at the top of our industry," he said.

"My team is looking for someone highly skilled in mathematics who can help to calculate the probabilities of specific events."

"Can you give me an example?" said Gwen.

"Certainly," said Mr. Bromwell. "My team recently calculated the probability that a woman would be home when an assassin came for her."

"Wow. That is really specific," said Gwen. "Can you tell me how you used the information?"

"Having that information allowed us to plan for multiple outcomes," said Mr. Bromwell. "It enhanced the ability of our agents to respond effectively. And, it offered us the potential to adjust our approach should circumstances have changed."

"That's impressive," said Gwen.

"Talent and technology have contributed to the firm's success," said Mr. Bromwell. "An internship with the firm would give you real-world experience in participating in the solutions to similar problems. You would work with a highly-rated team of statisticians."

"Mr. Bromwell, it sounds fascinating," said Gwen.

Mr. Bromwell smiled. "Very good," he said.

"Can you tell me the next steps in the process?" asked Gwen.

"Certainly. Please send an e-mail to the address on the back of my business card," said Mr. Bromwell. "My assistant Krista will get you set up for the summer."

"Wait," said Gwen. "Are you offering me the internship?"

"Yes, I am," said Mr. Bromwell. "Do you accept?"

Gwen glanced at the business card.

"Yes, I accept," she said. "Thank you."

"Welcome aboard, Ms. Prince," said Mr. Bromwell. "Thank you for the conversation."

ABOUT THE AUTHOR

Elaine Noone was born in New York City. She spent her career in the market research industry. *Coincidence* is her second novel.

www.ingramcontent.com/pod-product-compliance
Lightning Source LLC
LaVergne TN
LVHW091045080826
845145LV00002B/626

* 9 7 8 0 9 8 2 8 2 6 5 1 5 *